AMBUSHED BY LOVE

CAMP FIREFLY FALLS BOOK 21

ZOE YORK

CAMP FIREFLY FALLS BOOKS

WELCOME TO CAMP FIREFLY FALLS

Are you ready for the summer? Camp Firefly Falls, a sexy sleepaway summer camp for grownups is ready for you...

We are thrilled to announce a connected series of "escape from real life" stories set at Camp Firefly Falls, a fictional sleepaway camp for grownups, set in the Berkshires.

Visit our website at www.campfireflyfalls.com to see the latest releases and sign up for our special new release alert—we'll send you an email from camp every time there's a new book out!

OTHER CAMP FIREFLY FALLS BOOKS BY
ZOE YORK

Winning Back His Wife
Skinny Dipping Dare
Take a Chance on Me

www.zoeyork.com

ABOUT THIS BOOK

As a retirement gift, Rear Admiral Frank DeMarco has been gifted a week at an all-inclusive rustic resort in the Berkshires by his favorite Navy SEAL team. The VIP treatment is the last thing he wants, though. He has every intention to spend the week avoiding the other so-called Silver Fox campers—until one of them crawls into his bed in the middle of the night and he mistakes her for his late wife.

Grace Bennett knows better than to get involved with a man still clearly grieving the loss of his life-long partner. But there's something about Frank's gruff rejection of her that tugs at her heartstrings and makes her want to be his friend. And even though he claims he's not interested in her company, he keeps turning up everywhere she is, like a six-foot-three muscle-bound lost puppy.

Ambushed by Love is a lighthearted and sexy opposites-attract rom com from the author of *Skinny Dipping Dare* and *Take a Chance on Me*.

FOREWORD

I'm so glad you've discovered Camp Firefly Falls! I love this world. If you haven't yet read **Skinny Dipping Dare**, book 4 in the series, pick it up today—it's FREE! In it you meet Tegan Bennett and Wyatt Henderson, whose wedding is what brings Grace and Frank together in this book.

At least one of those books is always free, so visit my website at www.zoeyork.com and check them out if you haven't already!

I hope you enjoy Grace and Frank's story. I loved writing it.

I also have two stories about other couples in this series. *Take a Chance on Me* is Grady and Priya's story, and *Winning Back His Wife* started the whole thing off with Heather and Michael Tully and the Camp Firefly Falls origin story.

~ Zoe

ACKNOWLEDGMENTS

A grateful thanks to Jeremy, my new favorite editor, and Sherry, who suggested the title for this book

CHAPTER 1

ALWAYS TRUST YOUR GUT. That had been Frank's motto his entire adult life and had served him well up until a month ago, when he foolishly accepted a well-meaning gift from the Navy SEALs serving under his command.

Frank hadn't known what to think about the week of vacation in the Berkshire Mountains before the wedding of one of his favorite SEALs. An adult summer camp didn't sound like his kind of thing, but that's where Wyatt had met his bride, and it was where the wedding would take place next weekend.

In the end, he couldn't bring himself to decline the generous offer, so he'd flown out to the east coast a week early.

But from the moment Frank arrived in Boston, he'd wanted to turn around and fly right back to San Diego. The feeling intensified when he got on the Camp Firefly Falls shuttle bus the next morning and was hit by a wall of pheromones and testosterone-laden side-eye from people he assumed saw him as some kind of competition for the single women who easily made up half of his fellow adult campers.

Ha, he thought. *The joke is on you guys. I'm never getting laid again.*

Which was a damn shame, given that he was only fifty-seven and his equipment worked better than it had when he was twenty-seven.

It wasn't that he wasn't interested in sex, either. But his partner-in-crime on that front was gone, and he wasn't looking to replace her—ever.

The one-year anniversary of Bianca's death was barely behind him, anyway. Maybe one day, way down the road, he might…

His stomach twisted as he threw himself into a seat at the very back of the camp bus.

Nope.

Not even if he lived to be ninety-five. He'd jack it to the sweet memory of his wife bouncing on his lap. That would be enough. It had been everything, after all.

He flexed his hand and looked at his wedding ring.

This was definitely a mistake.

He appreciated what his team had been thinking—get the old man away from Coronado, away from his favorite haunts and all those memories of Bianca.

Frank dragged in a rough breath.

The first sign of trouble had been when the welcome package had arrived, highlighting the theme as Silver Fox week. Adult summer camp for the fifty-five-and-up set.

He glanced at the hormone-fest playing out in front of

him on the bus as they waited for the last few stragglers. The camp people should call it High School 2.0.

Well, Frank wasn't going to play any of those games. No drama, no making out under the bleachers.

He turned his hand over, revealing the tattoo he'd just had done on his forearm. A breast cancer ribbon wrapped around the nickname *Bia* in script. It had healed well, unlike his heart.

At the front of the bus, a camp staffer started counting heads.

Great, maybe they could get underway. He didn't care if they left anyone behind.

Unfortunately, the staff person didn't agree. "We're just waiting for Grace," he said pleasantly. "And then we'll be underway."

"That's me!" A blonde woman popped onto the bus, her backpack banging against the door as she waved her hand. "Sorry I'm late. I just wanted to grab some treats for the ride." She lifted her other arm and wiggled a plastic bag which bulged from cardboard boxes inside it. "Who likes canoli?"

Frank pulled his headphones out of his carry-on bag. He didn't like canoli, sunshine-y personalities, or blonde women in general. He'd lose himself in music just as soon as they got under way, which was thankfully happening now.

The camp staffer gave the word to the driver, and the bus started up. "I know everyone is eager to continue the socializing, so I'll keep this brief. As you know, this week at Firefly Falls is sponsored by the dating site *StarCrossed*..."

The rest of what the staffer said was lost in the dull but growing buzz in Frank's ears. *Dating site.*

How had he missed that? He wanted off this bus right the fuck now. But he wasn't going to make a scene. He swallowed around the giant lump in his throat, jammed his headphones onto his head, and sank as low in his seat as he possibly could get.

This was going to be the worst week of his life. He'd stick around for Henderson's wedding because he wasn't a jackass, but until his SEALs arrived, he was hiding from everyone.

GRACE STRETCHED her neck one way, then the other. She may have overdone it today with all her walking carrying that beast of a backpack. But she'd heard amazing things about a bakery in the North End, and the only thing that sounded worse than a two-plus hour bus ride with a bunch of strangers was the same without anything to eat.

Catching the bus from Boston to Camp Firefly Falls with the other campers had not been the plan. She lived north of the camp, on a hobby farm in upstate New York where she grew lavender and heirloom perennial flowers. When her daughter, Tegan, announced she was getting married at the camp, Grace had planned to drive down for the weekend.

But Tegan had different plans. She'd arranged for Grace to attend camp the week before the wedding as a so-called "treat" for the mother-of-the-bride.

Grace liked the idea of camp. She just wasn't sure how she felt about the theme of the week. She didn't feel like she was in her fifties most of the time. Ever since her divorce nearly twenty years ago, she'd felt like age had become nothing more than an abstract, meaningless number.

Or maybe that was simply her stubborn refusal to accept her ex-husband's toxic framing of aging as a bad thing. Regardless, she had mixed, complicated feelings about attending senior's week at camp, and while she enjoyed dating as much as the next single woman, she didn't have a *StarCrossed* profile like the people around her.

So, a week ago, she'd set out for a quiet road trip where she'd intended to end up in Briarsted and Camp Firefly Falls this weekend after some necessary solitude and reflection. But her car had broken down at an artisanal cheese farm in New Hampshire and she'd spent the last day and a half figuring out the best place to get it repaired without disrupting Tegan's wedding countdown.

The last thing she needed was to stress her daughter out with minor details like her car being stuck in Nashua.

She'd figure out how to get back to it after the wedding.

So she'd gone to a mall, bought the biggest backpack she could find, shoved everything she needed for camp into it, and hopped on a Greyhound to Boston, where she knew she could get on this bus, which she'd wanted to avoid in the first place.

But that was Grace Bennett's life in a nutshell. No matter what she did, she could never dodge the lemons. Every internet meme about life's hard lessons making one stronger both spoke to her and infuriated her at the same time.

Therefore, once she'd arrived in Boston, she squeezed in some sightseeing because, hello, it was *Boston*, and how often did she go on an adventure like this?

Lemonade. She was a pro at mixing it up nice and sweet.

"Canoli?" She smiled brightly at the woman sitting behind her and held out the first box. "Pass them back. I bought enough for everyone."

She handed the second box to the gentleman across the aisle from her, then she sank into her seat and let herself breathe.

In and out, focusing on her heart rate. In a few hours, she'd be at camp. And then she'd find a stiff drink.

CHAPTER 2

IT TURNED out that Camp Firefly Falls, the rustic-luxury adult re-boot version, was a fantastic place to get totally smashed.

There were Silver Fox shots on arrival, served by a handsome young man with very broad shoulders. The drink was mostly tequila with a silvery ribbon of lemon liqueur running through it. She took a photo on her phone —making sure to capture the cute camp counsellor in the picture, too—before tipping her second one back.

Heather Tully, the owner of the camp, came over to introduce herself. "I understand you're Tegan's mother," the pretty blonde said.

Grace wiped a touch of lemony sugar from the corner of her mouth. Excellent first impression for the mother of the bride to make. "That's me."

"We're delighted to have you here this week. If there's anything I can do to make the next few days max-relax for you before the chaos of the wedding begins, just let me know." The camp director winked.

Grace laughed despite herself. "What did Tegan say?"

"Nothing. I just remember my own wedding. Like Tegan, my wedding was quite the, uh, opposites-attract event."

Her hippie child was marrying a military man, and that hadn't been where Grace's mind had gone. Now, though... She took a deep breath. "Oh, goodness, I hadn't even thought about that. Unless my ex counts, but he's just opposite. No attract there, hasn't been for two decades. But you're right, I'm going to need all my Zen to negotiate a weekend with Navy people."

From behind her, there was a grunt. She turned around and caught a stern profile before the man stalked away.

She turned back to Heather, who gave her a bright smile. "Did you get your registration packet?"

"Not yet." She'd gotten distracted by tequila. And young shoulders.

"Once you pick up your cabin assignment details, we have more drinks down at the boathouse before dinner."

Tegan had failed to mention just how much booze was a part of the adult re-boot of her childhood summer camp. Grace's daughter had come to Camp Firefly Falls the first year Heather re-opened it for adults. A lot of camp alumni had. Tegan had taken it to the next level, returning last year as recreation director.

But this year, she was simply a camper again, and only for the weekend. Now Grace's daughter's life was squarely on the west coast, where her husband-to-be was a Navy SEAL.

And Grace liked Wyatt very much.

It was just so far from Saratoga Springs. From Grace, and the sweet little hobby farm she'd made their own.

Hot tears threatened behind her eyelids and she shook her head. Nope. Of course she would cry on Saturday. Her baby was getting married. But until then? She was a single woman who hadn't drunk anything more exciting than peppermint tea in *months*.

She was going to the boathouse for the promised before-dinner drinks.

And if dinner was mostly liquid, that was okay, too.

Grace Bennett was cutting loose.

HOURS LATER, she was still quite happy with that decision, but in hindsight she should have paid more attention to the details at registration. She vaguely remembered handing her backpack to the handsome boy with the broad shoulders, and someone else giving her a packet with a cabin assignment in it. Then she…did something with that folder.

Her tote bag!

She'd shoved it in there.

Now she just had to find that, which was a challenge because there were three of everything anywhere she looked. And in the hours of drinking and smiling and laughing, she hadn't really made any new friends. Lots of acquaintances. A few who'd gotten on the bus in Boston called her Canoli Girl, which was fun. Weird, because she was fifty-four, but still fun.

But now as darkness settled more firmly on the camp, and people paired off with their roommates—which Grace didn't have—or frisky new friends—which Grace didn't want—she found herself standing on the wide verandah of the main lodge. Everything was swimming around her. Furniture, people, the pretty lanterns on the wall.

"Ms. Bennett, is this yours?" And just like that, her tote bag reappeared at the end of a muscular arm. In triplicate, but she trusted that at least one of them was the real deal.

"Thank *you*," she said, wiggling her index finger in the general direction of his muscular chest. She wasn't entirely sure she pulled off the casual acknowledgment. So she added a super bright grin. *Oh, way to play it cool, Grace.*

Tegan hadn't told her about the booze, or the muscles. Hopefully by the end of the week she'd have gotten over her amazement at both. It wouldn't do for her daughter to know she was so easily impressed.

She yanked out the registration packet, ignoring how the words swam in front her eyes. She didn't need words. Just a cabin number.

And a map.

Maybe some good luck, too.

And because it had been a pretty good day, she found both. First a map, which was easy to read and follow, and then the excellent luck of her cabin being a straight shot down a path just to her left.

The moon lit her way, and before too long she found the right cabin. It was bigger than she expected, with a wide porch and a squeaky screen door.

Inside, she couldn't find a light switch.

Oh, sweet baby Jesus, maybe there was no electricity in the cabins. She racked her brain, trying to remember what Tegan had said about roughing it in luxury. Was no electricity compatible with lux accommodation?

Her head swam in confusion, and she decided that could be tomorrow's question to answer.

She looked around for her backpack, helpfully delivered by one of the handsome muscle men, but that was missing with the electricity. Maybe there was a dressing room she couldn't find in the dark.

Maybe she was drunk.

Yes, oh Lord, she was definitely drunk.

Time for bed, Grace.

Luckily the bed was in the middle of the room, big and covered in fluffy bedding. Relatively visible compared to the darkness of everything else. She zeroed in on the edge of it as she kicked off her shoes.

Whoa, that was hard. She wasn't even going to worry about her clothes. Better to leave them on than find herself on the floor, banged up because she couldn't work a button hole. She bumped against the mattress and tumbled forward, rolling under the blanket—and straight into a big, hard body, heavy enough to be weighing down the mattress.

Panic zapped through her.

There was someone else in her bed.

"Bia," the body rumbled, its voice warm and sleepy. Male. "Come here, baby. Lemme hold you. I'll be gentle."

Hands grabbed her—*hey, buddy, that's not exactly gentle as advertised*—and hauled her into the dip in the mattress before she could respond. But as soon as she stopped moving and the body shifted, a heavy weight against and around her, she responded like a demon spawn.

"Get off me!" She shoved hard, but inefficiently, and then scrabbled for a better…anything. Hold, leverage point, something to bite. She wasn't picky.

She was in bed with a stranger and he was ten seconds away from—

His hand slid under her shirt and his fingers splayed wide across her bare skin.

—groping her.

Too late.

"Stop. Fire. *Fire!*" Why didn't that work? "Hey, buddy, wake the hell up! I'm not Bia."

The body froze.

A long, agonizing beat stretched wide, then he was gone, shoving away from her as he jumped out of her bed.

She was about to follow him with more indignant yelling when she realized he was…not crying, exactly. But something.

Groaning.

Swearing, in an agonized way.

Besides, she wasn't sure she could leap out of bed in the same agile way he did.

Oh, was he was one of the muscle men? Damn it, she'd

been so focused on not being molested that she'd forgotten how youthful some of the men around here were. Youthful, nimble, and…still moaning.

Maybe he'd wounded himself on the way out of bed.

"Are you okay?" If he was, her next question was going to be if he knew where the light switch was.

But he didn't answer.

"Don't tell anyone about this," he rasped.

How could she? She still didn't really understand what this was. "Of course not." And then after another awkward, very silent beat, she added, "What were you doing in my bed?"

"It's my bed."

"But this is my cabin."

"Clearly not."

Was it clear? Nothing felt clear. Her head started to pound, and she wiggled herself off the bed, the opposite side from him. "I'm going to go."

"Where?"

"My cabin."

"You thought this was your cabin."

"But it's *clearly not*, as you just said."

"Why did you think this was your cabin?"

"Because I have the packet in my bag," she explained dumbly. "From registration."

"Show me."

"What?" She stepped toward the door, blindly reaching for her tote bag. Her hand came up empty.

The man had better luck. He swung it in the air. Maybe

he wasn't three sheets to the wind, or he had the night vision of an owl. Maybe both. Damn, to be sober and sharp-eyed.

"That's mine."

"You're drunk," he said slowly.

"Uh…" She took a deep breath. "That's none of your beeswax."

He chuckled.

Laughed.

He'd been nearly in tears before, then he'd asked her to keep that a secret—which of course she would, she was a nice person—and now he was laughing at her? She didn't think he knew how this empathy thing worked.

"Don't make fun of tipsy people," she said sourly. "It's not nice."

"You're swaying on the spot, lady. How about I help you find your cabin?"

"How about you help me find my tote bag?" She swiped at it and missed. "Hey!"

He reached in and pulled out the papers she'd looked at. "See?"

"Oh, I see." He turned them around. Like she could see anything. He knew she couldn't. "These are mine. You must have picked them up off the registration table. I didn't take them with me, I just memorized my cabin number."

"So, where's my cabin?" She may have shrieked the question, but ten-thirty at night was not the time to realize you didn't know where your bed was when you turned into an inebriated pumpkin.

And sleeping with the angry, sad man was not an option.

Maybe he could sleep on the floor.

No. That was the tequila talking. Not helpful. She took a deep breath and ground the heel of her hand into her left eyeball. "Think, Grace."

"You're Grace?" He chuckled again.

He needed to stop laughing at her. "Hey, buddy, you go to bed at nine o'clock at night, or whatever, so you can just suck it with the superior attitude, okay?"

"Okay, lady. Come on."

The next thing she knew, she was being propelled out of his cabin and away from the only bed she was sure she had access to tonight. But he didn't shove her far, just down the porch to a matching screen door. It turned out his cabin was one half of a cabin building, and there was another suite on the other side.

"I think this is your place," he said gruffly as he flipped on the light. "One of the staff members mentioned that my neighbor's name was Grace."

Sure enough, in the middle of the floor was her backpack.

Oh, yes.

She pumped her fist in the air and nearly toppled over, but firm, very sober hands caught her.

Oh, no.

A sinking, sobering realization skittered through her.

Angry, Sad Man was her next-door neighbor. And he thought—correctly—that she was a ditzy drunk.

That was it. Her camp career was over before it even began. What a complete disaster.

Damn.

CHAPTER 3

FRANK DIDN'T SLEEP AGAIN that night. He lay on top of the soft white quilt and let anger and self-loathing twist in his gut, not caring in the least that it wasn't a healthy way to deal with what had happened.

At one point he realized his face was wet, and he desperately wished he'd stolen a bottle of tequila from the main lodge. At another point he found himself face down, buried in the pillows, and he wasn't sure he wasn't silently screaming.

Just make it to the morning, he told himself. He'd sort his shit out then.

For now, he was wallowing in the stark, blinding grief of waking up to Not Bia in his arms. And the warped, upsetting feeling that his body hadn't cared, that his body had just been happy to have another source of heat to wrap around.

Heat, curves, sweetness.

As soon as he'd realized what was happening, he'd let

her go. But somewhere in there had been a millisecond when he'd wanted to keep holding the faceless, nameless woman because she felt good against him.

And he fucking hated himself for that.

In the morning, he'd get that under control.

For now, though, the train was pulling into Loathing Central in his head, and he didn't give a damn if that wasn't a good idea.

GRACE WOKE up full of regret—and that was before she tried to roll over.

Oh, Jesus, her head.

She was never drinking ever again.

Why was she up, anyway? It was... She lifted her eyes just enough to gingerly search for a clock.

No clock.

No clue what time it was.

The light streaming in the window wasn't blazing yet. And then in the distance she heard a bell. Maybe that was what had woken her up. Breakfast call.

She didn't want to eat anything. She wanted to stay in bed and think hard about what she'd done.

"Ms. Bennett?"

She groaned at the sound of the voice from outside.

It was followed by a knock.

Go away, she thought about saying, but that wasn't in the camp spirit. "Yes?"

"Breakfast hours have begun," someone said, far too

cheerily. "And Heather is going to do her welcome to camp spiel in half an hour. Orient everyone to the day's activities."

That didn't sound optional. Well, it was, of course, but only if Grace wanted to skip the rest of the day.

Could she skip the entire week? Have sandwiches sent over until Tegan arrived Friday night?

And then what? You'll tell your daughter you got blitzed out of your mind, crawled into a man's bed, kind of enjoyed the way he felt you up until it got weird and awkward, and then...you chickened out of life?

Right. No, she wasn't going do that.

"I'm up," she called out. "Thank you. I'll be there soon."

It took her twenty-five minutes. A hot shower, a clean change of clothes, and a loose bun for her still-damp hair made a world of difference.

By the time she got to the dining hall, most people looked like they were finishing up their breakfast. She quickly walked down the buffet line, grabbed a croissant, a couple of sausages, and a few orange slices.

What she really wanted was coffee.

And just like that, a carafe appeared in front of her, attached to a nicely muscled arm. Seriously, where did Heather Tully find all these handsome young men? She followed it—him—to a table.

It was only after she gratefully thanked him for the coffee that she realized she was two tables away from the Angry, Sad Man who was also her Next-Door Neighbor.

The two labels blared like car horns in her head. Extra-loud warnings she didn't need, because she saw him. He hadn't seen her yet, though. He was reading something on his phone, his jaw tense and his plate empty.

She shoved some croissant in her mouth and got a better look at him now. Everyone here this week was in their fifties, although he wasn't built like any middle-aged man she'd ever seen before. He was big and solid, like a tank, and he had a short hair cut like...

She choked on her croissant.

He had a short haircut like Wyatt, her soon-to-be son-in-law.

This man was military, she was sure of it.

She pulled out her own phone, not caring at all that it was only five in the morning on the west coast where her daughter currently was.

Grace: SOS from camp, daughter-of-mine. Any Navy SEALs here early for Silver Fox Week?

Tegan didn't reply. So Grace swallowed another chunk of croissant, chased it down with coffee, and texted Wyatt. It was an emergency, after all.

Grace: Hi Wyatt. Can you tell Tegan I texted her?
Wyatt: Morning, Grace. How's camp?

Clearly he hadn't picked up on the emergency vibe from her be-cool text. She abandoned all pretense.

Grace: Eventful so far. I had an awkward exchange with another camper last night.

Wyatt: Fistfight eventful or wore-the-same-dress eventful?
Grace: I had a few too many drinks and crawled into the wrong bed.

He didn't reply right away. That was probably the wrong thing to text your son-in-law. She was shit at this whole thing. When her phone lit up a few moments later, she was relieved to see her daughter's name on the screen.

Tegan: Mom, I'm up. Sort of. Wyatt's making me coffee. What did you do?
Grace: It's a long story. Do you have an answer to my question about Navy SEALs being here, maybe?
Tegan: Oh no. Mom, tell me you didn't.
Grace: Who is he, baby?
Tegan: Oh, shit. MOM.
Grace: WHAT? I DON'T KNOW WHAT I DID.

She took a surreptitious picture and texted it to her daughter.

Grace: WHO IS THIS?
Tegan: His name is Frank. He's the retiring base commander.
Grace: So, he'll be at the wedding?
Tegan: Oh yeah.
Grace: Great.
Tegan: That's not all.
Grace: Even better. Hit me with it all.

Tegan: He's a widower.

Bia. The wounded, aching sound.

The pit of Grace's stomach fell away, hollowing out the inside of her body. *Oh, shit* was right.

Tegan: Mom?
Grace: I'll fix this.
Tegan: Maybe don't do anything.

On the other side of the room, Heather Tully climbed onto a chair and hollered a cheery greeting as she held a piece of paper in the air. "Good morning, campers! Did everyone get their schedule for the day? Each morning this will be delivered to your cabin—" Grace had clearly missed that in her rush to get to breakfast. "But it's also posted in the main lodge, outside the dining hall, and today we have extra copies here as well. Raise your hand if you need one."

Grace didn't bother. She'd scurry back to her cabin at the first opportunity and look at it there in the safety of her solitude.

Heather continued. "Also, take a look to your left and right, folks. This is the highest enrolment of singles in any of our camp sessions." She said it with a nudge-nudge, wink-wink tease in her voice, and everyone shifted in their seats, an excited murmur rising from the crowd.

Jeepers, you'd think none of these people had been laid in the last year.

Grace tried to hide behind her coffee mug.

"You're going to be making new friends all week, and today's activities are all designed to help with that."

No, no, oh God, no. The noise level bumped up another notch as prime candidates were eyed up lasciviously, and Grace realized her mug wasn't going to protect her.

Get a grip, Grace Bennett. You can—

"You'll need a buddy for kayak lessons, macramé in the Arts and Crafts building, and then at lunch, we're going to do picnics for two out of the boat house!"

Nope. She could not do a picnic for two. Forced romance was a fate worse than death. Maybe kayaking. Kayaking sounded safe... But who would she be willing to get in a boat with?

Apparently, she wasn't alone in turning her head to check out the Navy SEAL commander two tables over. Grace watched in a mix of horror, shock, and black amusement as all the women in the room honed-in on Angry, Sad Neighbor. *Frank.* Wyatt's boss, so-to-speak, and a *widower.*

Maybe not all the women in the room. Eighty-six percent of them. There were a few in the back who couldn't see him, couldn't see how the way he was built like a concrete wall.

She knew firsthand how powerful his body felt. He would be an excellent partner for kayak lessons. And he could carry twenty picnic baskets at once.

This was a disaster.

She tapped her phone. Tegan had told her not to do anything, but...

Grace: Little late for that, baby. But don't worry. I'll make it up to him.

Tegan: I can fly out tomorrow if you need me.

Grace: I'm fine. Go back to sleep and dream of wedding things.

She wasn't fine, truthfully. She was still mortified about last night. But her neighbor had looked devastated last night, and right now he looked like he might blow a gasket any second. In the hierarchy of emotional need, he won. Or lost, as it were. Either way, she didn't have any business feeling sorry for herself. She took a deep breath and stood up, picked up her coffee, and pointed herself in his direction.

FRANK NOTICED in his peripheral vision as his flaky blonde neighbor approached. At least she didn't seem drunk this morning. Frazzled, but not intoxicated.

Good for her.

He didn't look up until she came to a nervous, skittish halt next to his table.

"I'm Grace," she said with more resolve than he expected.

"I know who you are. And I know you took my picture a minute ago."

Her cheeks turned pink. "Oh."

"Why'd you take my picture?"

"It's a long story. But what it boils down to is I want to

apologize for last night."

"That's not necessary."

"Okay." She sat down across from him.

That wasn't necessary either. He frowned.

She smiled brightly, pushing through her nerves. "Do you want to go on a picnic?"

"No."

"Good. Neither do I. But we're both about to be part-nered up with people who do, so...hello, partner. Let's dodge out of things together. Officially."

"Officially?"

"Unofficially, we'll go our separate ways as soon as humanly possible."

Frank was used to a lot of weird shit. The navy was super political once you got to a certain rank. He had batshit insane neighbors who had rules for maintaining the so-called "character" of Coronado Beach. Bianca's family had driven him nuts with expectations for reunions and holidays.

But he didn't know what to make of this woman. This...Grace.

She'd annoyed him on the bus and at registration. Canoli Girl didn't like military types, and that was before she'd crawled into his bed and sent him spiralling hard into grief again.

That's not on her. No, it wasn't.

But three strikes and you're out, lady.

"Listen," she whispered, leaning in. "I, uh... The thing is—"

"Excuse me," another woman said, stopping beside their

table and interrupting Grace. "You look like a man who knows his way around a canoe."

Swift boats were more his speed, but he could probably do anything with a paddle. "I'm afraid of water," he heard himself saying. Great, sixteen hours into camping and he was already a liar.

The woman didn't care. "How about lunch, then?"

She was pretty. Dark-haired like Bianca, curvy in all the right places. Also like Bianca. Tall, like—

"He has a picnic partner already," Grace said before taking a loud sip of coffee. She stared, unblinking, at the other woman until she turned and left.

"I do?" Frank asked her, feeling gruff and out of sorts.

Grace rolled her eyes. "Not really. Focus. I'm here to be whatever kind of beard you need."

"I don't need a beard. I handled that just fine." He frowned. "Didn't I?"

"You had a lost look on your face and spent four seconds too long checking out her cleavage. She was going to hook you somewhere along the way."

She thought he'd been checking out that woman? Oh, boy howdy was she wrong, and he told her as much.

Grace wasn't deterred. "You didn't *not* check out her cleavage," she said. "Which is fine. Boobs are great. But the boobs here are looking for rings and 401ks."

Boobs are great. What a thing for a stranger to say over breakfast. He took a deep breath. "That's cynical."

"That's me." She held out her hand. "Let me properly introduce myself. Grace Bennett. Mother of Tegan Bennett, bride-to-be."

Ah, for fuck's sake. Frank sighed as he shook her hand, his brain playing catch-up as he quickly re-organized his assumptions about this strange woman. He'd only met Wyatt's bride-to-be twice, but now he could see the resemblance. "So that's what this is about? You're worried the wedding will be awkward because of a bit of a misunderstanding." And the fact that Frank hadn't been friendly in the least.

"Yesterday wasn't my finest hour. And when I realized you must be here because of Wyatt, and we're going to spending all week together in some capacity…I just wanted to do my part here."

"No need to apologize. It's water under the bridge." Frank picked up his coffee. "So you were roped into this week, too?"

"A gift from my daughter."

He toasted her with his mug. "A gift from my entire team. A few of them have come here over the last two years, and they thought it was my turn, that I could do with some peace and quiet."

She laughed. "And then I happened."

"And then you happened." The right side of his mouth lifted in an almost-smile. "You think I need you to run interference for me?"

Her gaze raked over him, shrewd and knowing. "I doubt you need anyone to do anything. But you also seem a bit…this isn't your scene."

"You just said it wasn't yours, either."

"No, but it's closer to mine. If I squint, I like a lot about this place."

He could appreciate that. If he were in a different head space, or here with Bianca, he could probably enjoy it, too. "Don't let my black mood affect your fun this week, Ms. Bennett."

She made a face. "Please don't call me that. I'm Grace. Just Grace."

"My apologies. Grace, I appreciate your offer. And deflecting the first wave of attacks, as it were. But I'm..." Now it was his turn to pull a weird expression. It reflected the weirdness he felt inside. "I'm a mess. I lost my wife a year ago to cancer, and as you saw last night, I'm not over that."

"Of course not," she said softly. "I can't imagine."

No, she couldn't. Nobody could. He nodded gruffly. "So, you can understand why I'm not doing macramé."

Her lips twisted at how he said it. "Do you even know what it is?"

He was pretty sure it was something knitting-adjacent. Didn't matter. "It's something I won't like."

"That's...probably accurate." Grace took a deep breath, and Frank was almost amused by the restraint she was exhibiting. Officially, he was still grumpy.

Unofficially, he liked the way Grace had decided she was his bodyguard.

He didn't need protection. But it had also been a solid forty years since anyone had thought he did, and it was oddly endearing. There was something about Grace Bennett, like she might actually be...a friendly face over the next week.

Frank had a lot of acquaintances. He had a couple of

blood brothers from service. And he'd had Bianca for thirty years. He hadn't needed friends, not really.

And now here was this woman. Flighty, emotional, half-cocked in almost everything she did as far as he could tell, but also damn earnest and intent on redeeming herself for behavior that really didn't need redemption.

He should tell her that. Soon. Right now, she was throwing herself on an emotional grenade for him and he was pretty sure it made her feel better, so he'd let her continue.

"And I'm guessing you don't want to do kayaking or a picnic for two," she said.

"Correct on both counts."

She took a deep breath. "Well, if anyone asks, feel free to throw my name out there as your activity beard. And I guess, uh, well, I'll see you around."

She pushed away from the table and headed straight for the door. He watched her go. He didn't feel anything inside. She thought he'd been checking out that other woman's breasts? Ha. If he were going to check anything out, it would be the curve of Grace's bottom in her shorts or the pale stretch of her legs.

But he wasn't. He was completely disconnected from the part of him that used to appreciate women for their shapes and curves and softness.

He was going back to the cabin to catch up on the much-needed sleep he'd missed out on the night before. And then he had big plans for the rest of the day. A hike, a beer, and a big, shady tree someplace quiet.

CHAPTER 4

IT TURNED out there were lots of activities for people to do on their own, too. There was a bulletin board at the entrance to the main lodge with the schedule posted on it, and there were alternative activities for introverts.

Grace approved heartily.

It had taken her a long time to figure out that even though she had a social side, at her core she was very much a loner. More to the point, she preferred to do things on her own. She'd hated being married. Constantly needing to discuss and compromise, settling on something neither party was happy with—no wonder the marriage only lasted long enough to give her the world's most perfect child.

Then her ex had moved back to the city and left her to her own devices, which she poured into a life that actually made her happy without reservation.

What would make her happy today?

She picked a yoga class mid-morning, then a brief wild-flower identification lecture right before lunch. Maybe she would head to the boathouse in the afternoon for kayaking, safely after the partnered watercraft activities of the morning were well and truly over with.

As the hours ticked by, she found herself glancing around, wondering if Frank was doing anything. If he'd been coerced into a picnic, although she didn't see him on the lawn before she went to the dining room.

He wasn't there, either.

After lunch she headed to the lake and got a quick set of pointers on the basics from the boathouse staff.

"It's pretty easy," said yet another handsome young man, flashing her a ready smile. "As long as you don't mind getting wet."

She gave him an innocent smile. "I don't mind at all."

He didn't miss a beat. "Feel free to take your clothes off in the boathouse."

Giggling, she headed inside and quickly changed into her swimsuit, then picked one of the provided life jackets off the wall. Safety first.

Back at the dock, she watched the young man demonstrate how to get in and out of the kayak, then did her wobbly best to mimic what he did. Water sloshed into her seat. He was right. She was going to get soaked as she did this, but she was in the slim boat and surely that would be the hardest part.

Except she was wrong.

Paddling wasn't that bad. She figured out how to

roughly go in a straight line, and even got around raft tethered in the middle of the lake.

But once she was pointing back to the shore, everything seemed suddenly more precarious. The wind had picked up, pushing small but persistent waves against the side of her kayak. Even though it wasn't the direction she wanted to go in, it was easier to turn parallel to the shore and cut across the lake, across the waves.

And that was when she saw Frank.

He was sitting on a picnic table under a giant oak, all by himself, on the far side of the boathouse. He had a bottle in his hand and another one beside him. Not enough to get drunk and climb into the wrong bed, she thought to herself, so really, she had no leg to stand on in noticing that.

And she wasn't really sure why she did notice him anyway. He was a small figure in the distance. But in their handful of encounters, he'd made an impression on her. She was quite sure—and quite surprised to realize—that she'd recognize his large frame anywhere.

Uh oh.

That was unsettling.

She turned away from him. Better to figure out how to battle the waves than sit with those thoughts for a second longer. She could only imagine how that set of text messages would go down.

Grace: Confession time. I have started looking for Wyatt's boss at every turn and by the end of the

week, he'll be entirely sick of me. The wedding is
going to be amazing, though.
Tegan: Mom...

That was enough to make sure she didn't look back again. Her daughter loved her, Grace knew that. But there was always a thread of concern about her decision-making skills, especially when it came to men.

She headed out past the raft, because that was easier than returning to the boathouse. At this rate, she'd paddle straight across the lake and need to be fetched by a staff person, so she needed to tackle turning again.

Easy as pie.

Any second now.

"Having trouble?"

Twisting at the waist with a start, Grace dropped one end of her oar into the water. When she saw Frank in a kayak behind her, she squeaked and tried to recover, which only pulled her back alongside the rocking waves.

And then she overcompensated and somehow spilled over the other side of her kayak into the cool, wet darkness of the lake.

With a frustrated kick, she burst back through the surface of the water, sputtering. Right in front of her floated her oar. Beyond that, her kayak sailed majestically upside down.

Heart pounding, she glanced around.

Frank was on the other side of her kayak. She had a minute to compose herself. Thank goodness for her life jacket. She could just hang there in the water and pretend that whole embarrassing flip hadn't just happened.

"Grace?" He slid into view, his kayak cutting through the water faster than she could catch her breath.

"I'm fine."

"Take a minute to sort yourself out. Everything floats, you're in no rush."

"No rush for what?"

"Getting back in your kayak."

She laughed weakly. "Sure. Okay. I just learned how to use one of these ten minutes ago."

"I know, I was watching you. You did great."

"Until I capsized."

"That was on me. I startled you."

"Yeah, you did." She splashed water in his direction. He grinned.

"Are you going to help me?"

"Nope. You're going to help yourself."

Now was not the time for pep talks. "Frank—"

"You'll pull me in after you. Better for me to talk you through getting back into your kayak on your own."

She flailed around, looking for one of the hot, young lifeguards who wouldn't give her nearly as much grief, but she and Frank were too far from shore. Besides, they'd take one look at Frank and understand he had the situation in hand. "New plan. I'm going to swim back to shore, you push my kayak back for me, okay?"

He laughed.

On the one hand, she liked to see him grinning and

laughing. On the other, she'd prefer if they weren't at her expense. "Is this funny?"

"You're funny. This is just normal training for me."

"Spend a lot of time in kayaks, do you?"

His eyes crinkled at the corners. "How much do you know about your future son-in-law's job?"

"Let me guess. More swift boat, less kayak, but it's all the same."

"See? You're funny." He glanced around, then muttered something under his breath.

"Pardon?"

Instead of answering, he tipped himself sideways, flipping out of his kayak.

She swore, and it wasn't under her breath in the last. "Damn it, Frank, what are you *doing*?"

He probably only heard the last bit when he resurfaced, but he was grinning again.

Why did she like that so much? She barely knew the man.

Don't need to know him to be empathetic to his situation. Fair enough. So it was nice to see Sad, Angry Neighbor a little bit happy. And now soaking wet, and still happy. That was a sign of good mental health, surely.

He grabbed his kayak and his oar. Unlike the death grip she had on everything, he touched them loosely, keeping them close, but not appearing to worry about them floating away.

Maybe she should relax.

Maybe, but it wasn't happening.

ZOE YORK

"This is harder in the ocean, if that's any consolation," he said over his shoulder before flipping his kayak back right-side-up like it weighed nothing. "You do that with yours now."

"It's pretty hard in a lake," she muttered. Taking a deep breath, she relaxed her grip and tried to push the kayak over. It floated away a few feet—still face down. "See?"

"Try again, and this time, give it a pop."

She'd give him a pop right on the noggin. Rolling her eyes, she kicked over to her kayak and got her fingers under the edge. Pop, huh? Fine. One, two, three—

She heaved it up in the air and it flipped over like magic, none the worse for wear.

"That was just lucky." She looked over at him.

"Nothing to do with luck. Next step is to get up and on top of your craft. I'm going to do it first, and then you give it a go when you're feeling rested. No rush through any step. Once you get up on top of it, stay there and don't move."

"What do you mean, on top of it?"

He stretched one of his arms across the seat, to the far side of his kayak. "Like this." As if he had a portable trampoline under him, he burst out of the water like a dolphin, launching himself to lay across his kayak, tummy down.

Except Frank definitely didn't have a tummy. He had abs of steel—she imagined. *Don't imagine his abs,* she tried to tell herself. *Also, get the #@!*$ up on the kayak.* She didn't listen to either of those excellent suggestions. Instead she looked at her unlikely camp friend. Even in regular shorts and a t-shirt and soaking wet from a dunk in the lake he hadn't needed to make, he looked really good. Tight ass, long muscular legs. Those imagined abs, still bracing against his kayak. Took a lot of trunk strength to get himself up there, she bet.

He grabbed his oar and turned his kayak around so he could see her—and all in a single pull. "Everything okay over there?"

"Yep," she muttered. She dragged in a deep breath. Up and over and onto the kayak. She could do this. She had the advantage of a life jacket, after all. Easy-peasy-lemon-squeezy. She reached across to the handle on the far side and—

Up, she screamed in her head.

Her body didn't respond.

Unlike Frank, her upper body strength was that of a perfectly normal fifty-something-year-old. Namely, it was wholly inadequate for this particular task. "Nope," she said out loud. "Not going to happen."

"Scissor kick as you pull up. Don't make your arms do all the work. Your legs are much stronger."

She snorted, but tried it, and of course, he was right. She didn't get all the way up, but she got a pop. She sank back into the water, but not for long. With another deep breath, she tried again, and this time, she was up, and before the kayak could tip her—no thank you—she leaned her weight forward and flopped like a fish across her craft.

With her bottom pointed right at Frank.

And she wasn't wearing shorts.

Kill me now, she thought. She didn't mind her body in a bathing suit. Or out of it, for that matter. With the right person. Normal looking people her own age who also had average bodies. Not Sad, Angry "Defying Gravity Since 1985" Neighbor. Frank "How Many Chin Ups Can You Do? I Can Do More" Whatever His Last Name Was.

"How are you doing?" he asked.

"Just fantastic. Fan-fucking-tastic," she said, projecting her voice.

A couple who had just reached the raft looked in her direction.

She rolled her eyes as Frank chuckled behind her.

"Okay now I want you to think about flipping yourself over and twisting at the same time, ending up in your original seated position."

"Or back in the lake."

"Yep," he agreed. "That's a solid potential outcome here. But the good news is you already know what to do if you end up back in the drink."

At least he couldn't see her while she rolled her eyes. Flipping and twisting at the same time, huh? She lifted her head, then felt around with her hands. Maybe she could do it.

As she thought about it, he drifted into view again. Now he was upright in his kayak and his wet t-shirt was clinging to his thick, broad chest.

"Hi," she said brightly.

"Any time now, lady." He winked.

"Bite me, mister."

He laughed.

She took a deep breath, planted her hands on either side of her kayak and pulled her legs around as she lifted her upper body, twisting and flipping and making a lot of waves.

Much splashing. Not classy or dignified in the least.

But she was sitting in her seat—mostly—and was *not* back in the drink, as the Navy SEAL had so charmingly said.

"Well," she said briskly, grabbing for her oar. "That's enough of that for a lifetime. Now how do I get back to shore?"

CHAPTER 5

It took them fifteen minutes to get back to the boathouse, and Frank's cheeks hurt from smiling by the time Grace's kayak nudged the dock. One of the young guys was quick to help her out, and after she shot Frank a quick glance over her shoulder, she briskly headed inside.

He laughed again.

Sure, she was a newbie to paddling, but she'd handled it all with a hell of a lot of courage. And she was kind of adorable in her big-ass life jacket. She was just a little bit of a thing.

A little bit of a thing with a nice, curvy behind. He'd noticed it in an abstract way at breakfast, but when she was draped over the kayak out on the lake it had been harder to ignore.

He hadn't even tried not to look. It hadn't hurt anything, and it had felt kind of good to appreciate a woman's form.

Now he let himself have one last, surprisingly thirsty

gaze at her long legs and lovely hips, delightfully presented in the swim suit that peeked out from under the life jacket. Then he hauled himself out of the water and took care of stowing his kayak away.

"She did all right out there, didn't she?" The question came from one of the counsellors as Frank leaned his oar back in its spot on the wall.

"She sure did."

"You had good eyes. We thought, uh, she had more experience than that."

"She was fine," he said brusquely. He wasn't their commander. It wasn't his place to dress them down for the minimal instruction they'd given a total beginner. And Grace had a way of carrying herself that hid any discomfort.

He caught himself up short.

Huh.

Yeah, she did. And he'd spent yesterday thinking the worst of her for being manic and forceful, but she wasn't really either of those things.

Sarcastic, lippy, and pessimistic...she *was* all of those things. But he knew how to handle that kind of personality.

And he kind of liked it.

Grace stepped out of the boathouse, dressed again, her tote bag swinging loosely on one shoulder. The only sign of her adventure on the lake was her damp hair piled high on her head in a loose bun.

"What's next?" he asked, holding his hands wide.

She looked at him up and down. "Do you want to

change into something dry?"

"Nah, I'm fine."

"Are you sure?"

He shrugged. "We could find some drinks and sit in the sun for a while. There's a breeze. I'll dry out soon enough."

So that's what they did. They stopped at the picnic table he'd been sitting at when he'd realized she didn't know the first thing about how to paddle a kayak, and he grabbed the bottle of beer he'd abandoned. It was warm now, so when they got to the main lodge he traded it for a cold one.

Grace ordered a gin and tonic, with extra lime and extra tonic in a highball.

"Complicated order."

She smiled faintly. "I'm a complicated woman."

He learned more about how complicated she was over the rest of the afternoon, after they found a sunny spot behind the main lodge. Somehow, in short, self-depre-cating bursts, she revealed a bit about her divorce—mutual and a long time ago, but still a source of some understand-able resentment—and a lot about her life choices since then, which she'd learned to prioritize around the equal and hard-to-balance values of frugality and luxurious reward.

"I bet you've travelled a lot with the navy," she said as she sipped her drink. "Anywhere amazing?"

"More intense than amazing, although I always enjoy visiting Hawaii and Japan."

"Japan is on my list."

"Where have you gone so far?"

"Anywhere backpacking hostels are cheap." She

grinned, looking very youthful. Not younger than her age, exactly, but young for her age. "Belize was a favorite. Iceland was another, although that was only three days."

"Why only three days?"

"I got an insane deal on airfare two years ago, and those were the dates." She shrugged. "Better something than nothing."

But his favorite insight was around her rules for pizza toppings, because make-your-own-wood-fired-pizzas were on the dinner menu.

"Wait, let me get this straight," he said as he rolled his now-empty beer bottle back and forth between his fingertips. "You will eat pineapple on a pizza—in a pinch—but only with barbecue sauce and chicken, no ham in sight?"

"It's weird with tomato sauce."

He chuckled. "And the ham thing?"

"I'm just saying it's not really Hawaiian pizza. Did you know a Canadian invented it? To me, the true island taste is chicken and a spicier sauce."

"That is complicated. What are your rules around pepperoni?"

She grinned. "You'll find out at dinner."

"I guess so." He laughed. "Cliffhanger."

She stretched her arms high above her head. "Would you like another beer? It's almost happy hour."

He did.

But he also didn't. "I might take a break before dinner."

She nodded, her gaze already locked on the main lodge below them. "All right. See you later. I'm going in search of another G&T."

He walked her as far as the back door, then cut around and skirted along the edge of camp until he found his cabin.

But when he stretched out on his bed, he didn't like the silence.

He closed his eyes and tried to find some stillness in his thoughts. He failed miserably. Instead of peace, he had pain and confusion and, in an unexpected twist, some curiosity too. He wondered if Grace had already found a new drinking buddy at the bar.

What sort of insanity did *StarCrossed*-inspired campers get up to at Happy Hour?

He lay there for another fifteen minutes before giving up. He wasn't going for pre-dinner drinks. He was going to dinner, just a few minutes early. And if he found Grace again, well, he'd have someone to eat dinner with, which certainly wasn't the worst thing in the world.

Plus then he'd find out what her deal was with pepperoni.

He found her in the lobby of the main lodge, listening with obviously polite-but-not-genuine interest to a group conversation. Her nods were too regular, her gaze not sharp enough.

And when he walked in, her eyes flicked in his direction. She smiled and he returned the gesture.

She excused herself, and relief coursed through him.

"Hey," she said quietly as she came abreast. "Hoping to be first in the pizza line?"

"Damn straight."

She laughed, and just like that, he had a dinner date.

44

No, a dinner partner.

They headed to the dining hall and were the first through the doors when they opened. After setting their drinks on a table, they headed to the pizza stations. It was quite cleverly set up so multiple people could be assembling a pizza at once, which meant Grace disappeared around the far side of the station as he was building the world's best deluxe pizza.

When she returned, he realized her pepperoni quirk was in fact super weird.

And she was grinning because she knew it.

He looked at the pizza tray in her hand, then up to her face. "That's not how you assemble a pizza."

"Says who?"

He pointed to his own pizza, with all the ingredients evenly distributed. "Says everyone."

She shrugged. "Everyone is wrong. Pepperoni is hard to cut, and it falls off the tips of a pizza slice. It only belongs within an inch of the crust."

So he could see. Her pizza was concentric circles of toppings. Pepperoni around the perimeter, then green pepper, mushrooms, and finally onion in the center.

It was, technically, the same pizza he'd assembled.

But it was completely different. Just like Grace.

"Each bite only has one flavour to it," he said, still hung up on her design. "That's not how pizza works."

"No? We'll see. I'll let you have a bite once they're cooked."

They got in line for the ovens, and while their pizzas were baking, they loaded up their plates with side salads and garlic bread wedges. Once they were back at their table, she cut him a small piece of hers—and it was, in fact, delicious. Each bite was a distinct taste, but they built up, and when he finished, he eyed the rest of her pie.

"Do you want more? I won't eat it all." She took a big bite of her garlic bread and gestured for him to take another slice.

He did, but he set it to the side, and ate it last after consuming his more conventional version.

Hers was better.

He told her as much, and she smiled like she'd been given a gift.

AFTER DINNER, people spilled out onto the lawn, which ran down to the lake. There would be a bonfire after dusk, but for now, there was more drinking and flirting.

"Do you have a *StarCrossed* profile?" Frank asked as he watched Grace watch the rest of the campers.

She gave him a surprised look. "No. Why?"

"Just curious. I don't either." He felt his neck heat up. "Wyatt wasn't exactly clear on the fact that a dating app was sponsoring this week."

She made a face. "Sorry. I knew, but Tegan promised that part was optional."

"So far it has been, so I guess she was right."

"That must have been an unwelcome shock when you realized."

"It contributed to my grumpiness on the first day."

Her lips quirked. "You mean yesterday?"

"Jeez, was that only yesterday?" He barked a laugh. "Yeah. That."

"You've survived thirty hours of dating camp," she said with mock-solemnity. "Well done."

He dragged in a breath. "Thanks. Today wasn't so bad in the end. After breakfast, I thought the whole peace and quiet thing was a non-starter, but then I got to chill out, and *then* there was the whole fun kayaking thing…"

Grace laughed.

"And really, it's not like *everyone* is hooking up."

"Ah." Her tone gentled, like she knew romance was painful for him.

Frank did his best to ignore the sound. Sweet, soft. Understanding.

He hated understanding sounds. Had heard enough of them for a lifetime.

But then she squared her shoulders and gestured at the milling crowd in front of them. "Are you sure about that, though? Most are pairing up—and good for them."

"Sure, there's some of that," he said gruffly. But then he pointed at a pair of women at the next bench over. "But we're not alone in dodging the meat market."

Grace choked on whatever was going to come out of her mouth next. "Uh," she finally said, her voice raw. "Uh…"

"What?"

She turned her head and lowered her voice, her eyes sparkling. "They're totally hooking up, Frank. You know? With each other."

47

Well, damn. "Good for them," he muttered.

"There's nothing wrong—"

"Jesus," he spit out. "No, of course not. That's not how I meant that. Love is love. I've had lots of gay service members serve under me. Don't you think I have a problem with that."

"Okay." She nodded. "Good."

He sighed. He wasn't great company at the best of times, and now he'd made things awkward because he couldn't spot a lesbian at a thousand paces. "I'm going to head back to the cabin."

She hesitated, then nodded. "Have a good night."

He wouldn't. He didn't, ever.

It wasn't until he got back to his quiet, sad, empty bed that he realized he hadn't acknowledged her frustrated good night.

GRACE WATCHED FRANK STALK OFF, then slowly made her way to the main lodge. She needed a pot of chamomile tea. It was a stark contrast to the night before, but all in all, she'd take today over yesterday.

Tomorrow was a whole different story. She wasn't going to spend the whole day with Frank. He didn't need that, she didn't want that. She needed to find something to do on her own.

She found Michael Tully behind the bar.

"What can I get you?" he asked.

"I was hoping for a pot of herbal tea."

"Coming right up." He lifted a tray from behind the bar and set it out for her to choose. "Pick your poison. I'll be back with a hot water thermos in a minute."

She looked at the options and stuck with the chamomile she'd originally wanted.

When Michael returned from the kitchen, he had an insulated thermos in one hand and a mug in the other. "You can have it here, of course, but I thought you might want to take this to go. Chamomile is nicest when you're already tucked into bed, isn't it?"

Grace exhaled happily. "Yes it is. Thank you."

On her way to the exit she spied a bookshelf in the corner. A sign encouraged her to take a book, so she picked a lovely looking romance with a larger-than-life pirate on the cover.

But when she returned to the cabin, there was a larger-than-life SEAL sitting on her porch. Their porch. No reading just yet.

"I thought you were off to bed," she said, coming to a stop in front of the steps.

"You said good night, and I just stomped off. That was rude of me."

"It's been a long day. Don't worry about it."

He frowned. "Okay."

But he didn't move.

She held up the Thermos. "Do you want some tea?"

"Nah, I'm fine. Never been much for tea."

"It's chamomile."

He burst out laughing. "That doesn't make it better. I don't want to drink flowers."

She poked her tongue into the inside of her cheek and counted backwards from ten. She got to seven. "Are you always this much of a grumpy curmudgeon?"

He hesitated before nodding. "Pretty much."

"Wow."

"Are you always a predictable hippie?"

She gave him a rueful smile. "Pretty much."

"Well then, we're an interesting pair of neighbors." He shifted to the side. "Come and sit. Drink your tea."

She didn't bother to point out that he barked orders. He knew it, and she was going to sit anyway. So, she sat. She set her book on the step, and twisted the top off the Thermos. The immediate hit of floral warmth made her smile. Yep, she was a hippie. Yep, she liked flowery tea.

Frank picked up the paperback.

She poured herself a cup and waited for his gruff response to the pirate cover.

He didn't say anything.

When she glanced over, he was rubbing his thumb over the raised letters of the author's name. "My wife loved historical novels," he said. "She read these all the time. I think I have some by this author on my coffee table at home."

She didn't know what to say.

He looked sideways at her. "Sorry."

"Don't be. It sounds hard."

"It is. And it's also not something I'm supposed to wallow in so..." He set the book down. "I think you'll like that one. Bianca always did, anyway."

"Do you want to talk about her?"

"Always." He laughed hollowly. "But I don't want to be a conversation killer, either."

"You aren't. Did she like flowery tea?"

His laugh was more genuine this time. "No. We were both coffee drinkers. And cold drinks. She made a wicked lemonade."

"And now? What do you like to drink now?"

"Always coffee. Still and forever. I've discovered iced coffee. Cold brew. That's a whole new thing that happened while B was sick which I missed. She would've liked that."

"It's good stuff." She sipped her tea.

"How about you? What do you like?"

"Other than flowery tea? Coffee. Juice. Mmm, I love fresh-squeezed or fresh-pressed anything. Fresh apple cider in the fall is the most amazing taste. Maybe it's an east coast thing."

"Cider's good, yep."

The conversation faded there. Small talk. Empty, simple words. Meaningless. But they also weren't loaded with angst, which was nice.

After a bit, when her cup was nearly empty, she picked up the book. "Thanks for the recommendation on this author. I'm looking forward to reading it even more now."

He nodded. She stood up. She was almost to her door when he asked an unexpected question. "What are you doing tomorrow?"

She paused. "Not sure yet."

"Maybe we could try the kayaks again?"

Another beat. What harm was there in that? "Sure. Sounds good."

CHAPTER 6

FOR THE SECOND day in a row, Grace was woken up by the breakfast bell, followed by a knock at the door.

Today, though, the knock was a hard, unyielding tap against the frame. Not the happy bounce of knuckles by a camp staff person.

Nope, that was Frank, and she knew that before he even announced himself with a clearing of his throat. "Grace? You up?"

She shoved her blankets off her legs and padded over to the door in her pajamas. "Morning," she said as she pulled it open.

He gave her a tight smile. "Are you going to breakfast?"

"Looking for company?" Breakfast and kayaking would mean they were spending the whole morning together.

He hesitated. "I guess so. If you want company, that is."

She thought about it long enough that he got a sheepish look on his face. She couldn't handle that, so she held out her hand and touched his forearm. His skin was warm and tight in the early morning cool, and his muscles flexed under her fingertips. "Sure. Give me ten minutes to get ready?"

He nodded, and she gently closed the door, keeping her confusion off her face until she was alone again. In the bathroom, she sighed at herself in the mirror. What was happening?

She didn't know. And thinking about it too hard made her head hurt.

At breakfast, all the tables for two were taken, so they sat with a woman named Ruth who had to be in her eighties, although she was full of energy. She had big plans for a tennis lesson with Nate, which she raved about for most of the meal.

"If you want a lesson, you'll need to sign up soon," Ruth said.

"We've got kayaking this morning, but we'll put it on the list for later," Frank told her.

We? List? Later? Grace did a double-take as Ruth turned to flag down a waiter for more coffee. Frank winked.

That didn't help her confusion in the least.

After Ruth finished eating and excused herself, Frank leaned in. "Beard coverage goes both ways."

She couldn't help but smile at that. "Okay. Thanks for saving me from the agony of spending an hour with the hot tennis instructor."

He chuckled. "Come on, my friend. Let's go grab two kayaks before the rest of the campers steal the chance from us."

In fact, they had the lake to themselves. Grace was already wearing her swimsuit under her clothes, so she stripped down in the boathouse again and put on a life jacket. When she came out, Frank had two kayaks in the water next to the dock and two paddles waiting as well.

"All set?"

"As ready as I'll ever be," she said bravely.

But this turn on the kayaks went better than the day before. No tipping, and her paddling was getting smoother. She even returned to the dock relatively dry, enough that she could have left her shorts on if she didn't mind a bit of dampness.

"If you go out on the lake again tomorrow, you'll be a pro in no time," Frank said as they returned their gear to the staff.

You. Not them, just her. The need for cover was gone, and it was a good reminder that Frank was there to lean on —and she'd offered to be there for him to do the same—but he didn't really want to spend all his time with her.

He was miserable here, and just counting down the days until the wedding.

Speaking of which, that was where she should put her attention today. "I need to go find Heather," she said brightly. "She's officiating Tegan and Wyatt's wedding ceremony and I'd like to go over those details. Thanks for the company on the kayaks, and all the tips."

She skedaddled out of there before he could reply.

FRANK WAS PRETTY sure he spent more time watching Grace hustle away from him than was natural. And yet he very much liked watching her, so he didn't question it too much. There wasn't anything else to do around here, anyway.

That was why he'd sought her out for breakfast. And kayaking.

And if he were being honest with himself, he'd look for her at lunch, too.

Which…he might want to question that. The more he thought about it, her reactions to him today had been hesitant and careful. He'd practically had to drag her to breakfast and then kayaking. And at the first opportunity, she'd dodged away as fast as she could.

He was getting rusty at reading people. Or maybe he'd never been that good at it, and it hadn't mattered before.

He took a deep breath and headed to the main lodge. Maybe instead of leaning heavily on Grace for company, he could get some advice on a good, long hike to take. One that might clear his head and give his body some good, clean work to do.

At the activity board, he found hiking maps, and a bright sticker on the front advertised that the kitchen could prepare lunches to take along on the walk. He checked in at the main desk about that.

"Yep, we can do a brown-bag lunch, no problem. They're ready at eleven, you can come back then and pick yours up then. And in the future, you can put in an early morning pick-up request as well."

He knocked on the wood counter. That sounded like a great idea. "Can I do that for tomorrow?"

"Sure thing. For one person?"

He flicked a quick glance at the menu example on the pamphlet. It didn't sound like enough calories for him to do a full-day hike. He assumed most campers weren't him, though. "Can you make it two orders?"

"Of course."

He gave the man a grateful smile. "Thanks. I'll be back in a bit."

So, he had an hour to kill. He headed back to the activity board. Tennis lessons popped out at him, and he thought of Grace. Had she wanted to take lessons?

Bianca had played tennis four times a week her whole adult life. He'd enjoyed it when he'd had time. Maybe—

No.

He jerked his attention elsewhere on the board. Anything else but tennis.

Except everywhere he looked now, he saw his wife. Cooking classes in the kitchen, swimming races.

Even the Arts & Crafts lesson going on right now—friendship bracelets—reminded him of the embroidery thread Bia had bought for a Navy wives project. He'd thrown out the remnants just last month when he'd finally worked up the courage to clear out her craft room.

"It's so hard for the spouses, Frank. You'll never understand. Not really. I know it's hard for you when you go, but you have a purpose. And it's not really like you have a choice. I know what it's like to sit at home and feel...empty. Alone. Scared."

The thing was, he did understand. Now. Now that it

was too late, he knew exactly what his wife had tried to explain all those years ago. He'd been a young commander, full of drive and eager to lead his first overseas command in Afghanistan. It had been the early days of their engagement there. Ugly, chaotic, dangerous.

Back home, his wife had held a lot of scared hands.

He'd brought back all those men. Every single one of them returned alive, which was a miracle. Not every tour of duty was that lucky. Not every commander was able to protect his men, and those that couldn't weren't any less skilled at leadership than he was.

And his wife's doctors couldn't save her.

Grief welled up inside him and he blindly turned in the direction of the Arts & Crafts building. His legs churned as he stalked away from that pain. Not today, grief. Fuck off.

He was going to make a friendship bracelet or three and think about his wife's accomplishments. *Her* leadership, *her* athleticism, *her* friendship. To him, to other military spouses, to everyone she ever met.

She'd be best friends with Grace right now. They'd be taking tennis lessons from Nate together while Frank did a hike on his own. Even if Grace didn't want to, Bianca would have talked her into it, finding the angle that would please her new friend.

When he got to the class, he yanked the door open.

The space was empty. It was a big room, lit by tall windows on both sides. Tons of sunlight streaming in, and zero people anywhere to be seen, although the back of the room was dark. Maybe it was in another part of the building.

His heart pounded in his chest and his palms slicked with sweat. He swallowed around a lump in his throat.

Damn it, he'd really wanted to make a friendship bracelet. Or three.

"Hello?" A female voice, thick and husky called out from the shadows at the back of the room.

He lifted his hand to shield his eyes from the overly bright windows. As his gaze adjusted to the light, he realized a woman was walking toward him. Tall, stacked, brunette.

Bianca.

But when she stepped into the first spot of sunlight, his heart sank. It wasn't his wife. Of course it wasn't.

From the shirt, he could tell it was a staff person. She smiled at him. "You're the only person who showed up for the craft session. Sorry, I was just in the back getting organized for the next one. Dreamcatchers—hopefully they're more popular than bracelets."

He gave her a tight smile. "Hopefully."

"Come in, sit down. I'm Rachel." She waved her hand, and a diamond glinted on her left hand. "Is this your first craft session? Do you know the drill?"

"First time, yep."

"Okay, well I'm here to help."

He almost begged off, but she was already setting out trays. So he followed her to a table and sat across from her. Up close, she didn't bear much of a resemblance to Bia after all. A similar tone of voice, similar height, and they both had dark hair.

He gave his head a shake and focused on the task at hand.

At first the work was clumsy. His fingers felt too big to string the circular device, and the delicate embroidery thread kept getting tangled. But once he got the hang of it, with Rachel's guidance, he finished a bracelet.

"Not bad," she said, looking at his handiwork from across the table.

But not great. The start of it was looser than the end, where his pulls on the thread had gotten tighter. "Can I make another?"

"Of course. The same colors?"

He looked at the bracelet in his hand. He'd picked it because they were Bianca's favorite colors. Blue, purple, emerald green. Then he looked at the other trays. A pale periwinkle blue caught his eye. The other colors were yellow and orange. Summery and sweet, like Grace. "I'll make that one next."

"Lovely." She handed it over. "Do you remember how to start?"

"I think so."

She watched him carefully until he was under way. This one was smoother than the first, consistent from start to finish. He liked it a lot. When he finished, he looked at the clock. There was just enough time. "I want to fix the first one to look like this one," he said. "Can you help me?"

"Of course." Rachel came around to his side of the table and helped him unweave the first bracelet and get it re-loomed. "There you go."

"It's almost time for me to get my hiking lunch," he said. "Can I come back and finish this later?"

"You can take it with you, if you'd like. Bring the loom back any time this week."

He gave her a grateful smile. "Thanks."

After carefully folding up his project and putting it in his pocket, he went through the main lodge, grabbed his food order, and then headed back to the cabin to get changed for an afternoon on the trails.

But as he stepped onto the porch, Grace's door swung open.

They stopped at the same time.

It felt awkward for reasons he couldn't really put his finger on. "Hey."

She smiled politely. "Hello."

"Did you find Heather?"

"Yep."

Yes, definitely awkward. He took a deep breath. "I made you a friendship bracelet."

She blinked at him.

"I had an hour to kill, so I went to the craft building—it's a long story."

"Oh."

"Too weird?"

"No…" She crossed her arms over her chest. She looked small like that, and it poked at something deep inside. "It wasn't what I was expecting, that's all." She tilted her head so she could squint up at him.

He moved back and sat down on the step.

Slowly, she joined him, still looking at him with wary

curiosity. "Do you sometimes find it hard to navigate human relationships?"

He nodded ruefully. "Always."

"Shouldn't it be easier at our age? I see all these people —" She gestured toward the center of camp. "They all seem to understand the social rules. They're all excited to be here and pair up, and I'm counting down the hours until my daughter arrives, so I can bury myself in mother-of-the-bride stuff."

"How did your meeting with Heather go?"

She lifted her shoulders in a weak shrug. "It was five minutes of her reassuring me that they were having weddings all summer long here and they know what they're doing. Tegan and Wyatt have written their own vows and it's a short service. There's nothing else for me to really do."

"I'm sorry."

"Meh. It's fine." She looked at the bracelet in his hand. "That's really for me?"

"Yeah." He held it out.

"What's the longer version of the story?"

He took a deep breath. "I'm going for a hike this afternoon, and they're making me a bagged lunch. It wasn't going to be ready for an hour, so I went to the craft building." He skipped over the part about the emotional grief crisis. "My wife made these once for other navy wives. The first one I made was for her. When I get back to California, I'll take it to her grave and tell her about camp. Then I had time to make another one, and I thought these colors suited you."

"That's really sweet," she whispered as she took it in her slim fingers. "It's beautiful."

"I think we're going to get through this week together —" he said at the same time as she added, "I wasn't sure you liked me at all, to be honest."

They both stopped and stared at each other.

"Wait, what?" He leaned in, bracing his hand on the porch behind them. "Grace, I like you a lot. You're funny and smart and you seem to get me even though we're complete opposites. Why wouldn't I like you?"

"Uh…" She turned red. "It doesn't matter."

"It does." He frowned.

She licked her lips. "Why?"

"Because I don't want to push myself on you."

Her eyes got wide. "You think you're pushing yourself on me?"

"Isn't that what you thought? This morning? I dragged you to breakfast, I made you go kayaking, and then at the soonest opportunity—"

"I thought you were done with me," she whispered.

Something cracked in his chest. "No," he murmured softly. "Not at all."

She fiddled with the bracelet. "Oh."

"I'm glad I made that for you, then, because I want to be your friend, Grace. I want to learn more about flowery tea and your lavender farm and backpacking through Belize."

Her mouth bloomed into the nicest, sweetest smile, and he reached out and brushed his knuckles on her cheek. "There. That's better."

She laughed.

"That's a good sound."

"Yeah?" She turned to look squarely at him and suddenly they were very close.

His hand dropped away from her face and his heart thumped hard in his chest. She looked like pure sunshine. Warm and happy.

He hadn't felt the sun in so long. He could feel himself leaning in, and it felt good.

And then she breathed his name. "Frank." Or maybe it was a question. "Frank?" His brain couldn't process it clearly, but it was enough to trip him up.

He jerked back, and she did the same.

"Frank—"

"It's lunch time," he said gruffly. "I'm off for a hike. See you later?"

"Sure."

And then it was her turn to watch him stalk off.

CHAPTER 7

FRANK HEADED INTO THE WOODS, his lunch packed into a ruck on his back. His body creaked and protested at first, but once he got into the rhythm of the hike, it felt good to move. It felt good to be alone with his thoughts, too, in the regulated way they happened when he was in motion.

His grief counsellor had told him to go for a daily walk, which he'd laughed at pretty hard—he could run, he could sprint through an obstacle course, or bench press his weight and then some. He didn't need to *go for a walk*. It was so...simple. Too simple.

But like most advice from professionals, it actually worked. Once he'd pushed through his resistance, he'd found there was something in the slower pace, in the steady push of one foot in front of another, that did something to the overwhelming thoughts in his head.

Sorted his shit out, basically.

And this afternoon, he needed his shit to be sorted,

because he was pretty sure he'd almost kissed Grace, and that was *insanity*.

Pretty sure? What kind of fucked-up denial is that? Yeah. Right. He'd almost kissed Grace.

He'd *wanted* to kiss her.

He could still feel that nervous excitement in his gut as he'd leaned in.

Two days before he'd been scoffing at the idea of camp hook-ups. Now he was flirting with his next-door-neighbor and liking it. Or at least, liking it right up until the second it felt wrong, and then he ran away.

He shoved his hand into his pocket and closed his fingers around the friendship bracelet loom. *Oh, Bianca, what am I doing?*

There was never any answer when he spoke to her. She was gone, and everything she would say now, she'd said in the months leading up to her death.

"Don't you die on me, too, Frank. Find your way back to a new life. Promise me."

He had promised her. But he hadn't given her any time-line for a reason. He was pretty sure he was going to spend the rest of his life with a hole in his heart, and any life that managed to pulse around that was a miracle.

He tried to tell the Bianca in his head that he'd almost kissed someone else. He couldn't do it. As soon as he tried to put the words together, she shimmered away.

As he walked on, he cycled through all of those thoughts again and again, looking at them from all different directions. He shouldn't be thinking about Bia if and when he kissed someone else anyway.

When he got to the top of the trail head, in an open clearing, he turned around and looked down the mountainside toward camp.

If and when he kissed someone, he'd have to be sure about it.

Swinging his pack off his back, he looked for a spot to eat his lunch. And then he was going to re-make his Bianca bracelet and mull over what it might feel like to be sure about something.

IT WAS WELL past dinner by the time he returned to camp. That was fine. He had some snacks in his room.

Grace's side of the cabin was dark, and he thought about going in search of her, but the conversation he wanted to have couldn't happen at the boathouse or around the bar in the main lodge.

Instead, he decided to leave her a note.

But while he was hunting for paper, and then a pen, she returned. He heard her footsteps outside and dropped the pad of paper he'd found, wanting to catch her before she went into her room.

She turned and looked at him when he burst onto the porch. "You're back."

"Yeah." There wasn't much light. Just the stream coming from his door, and she was in shadows, closer to hers. It was hard to read her.

"How was the hike?"

"Good enough. I needed to clear my head. Any trail would have sufficed."

"Frank—"

"I'm sorry." He barked it out. Not a great first take. "And I'm sorry for saying it like that, I guess." He rubbed his jaw. "You've been kind to me."

She moved closer. "You don't have anything to be sorry for. You told me that after I crawled into your bed and made a fool of myself. Now it's my turn to give that back. We're all human. And we get drunk, we reach out, we..." She threw her head back and sighed. "We sometimes do stupid shit."

It hadn't been stupid. Simply premature. "Do you ever not swear?"

"Says the guy in the navy?" She looked back at him, her eyes twinkling. "Fuck no."

He laughed with her. Then he sobered up again. "But seriously, Grace. I think we cleared up some confusion earlier, only for me to muddy those waters again."

"Frank...if you had kissed me, that would have been okay, too. I've been single for twenty years. I kiss a lot of frogs. I know it doesn't mean anything, and sometimes it feels good. Don't overthink it."

He wasn't overthinking it. Not anymore. He'd spent all afternoon thinking, and reasoning, and trying to come up with any plan other than getting his mouth on hers.

GRACE HAD THOUGHT that would be the end of it. Re-frame

the lean-in as something normal and inconsequential. Promise it meant nothing and move on.

But Frank didn't step back. In fact, he moved in closer, and this time there was none of the nervous energy zinging off him that there had been earlier. This man was more like a predator, coiled tight and ready to pounce.

And like she was his prey.

She knew this feeling, too. It was rarer than the frog kissing. There had only been a couple of guys over the years who had been this…intense. And it was dangerous, because she liked intense. Deep down, intense was her jam, and no no no, Frank could not be her jam.

"You know what I've learned, Grace?"

She swallowed. *Don't fall for it.* She fell for it. "What?"

"Life is too short to be polite, or demure, or anything other than balls-to-the-wall."

"That's me. One hundred percent to the wall with my—"

He reached out and cupped her face, his thumb rubbing against her lips.

She fell silent. They weren't bitching about the state of the world. He was talking about… She watched him move closer, his eyes bright and his jaw set. Yeah, he totally wanted to kiss her now.

And that was great, except for all the ways it was still a terrible idea. No big deal, but still nope. She stepped back, bumping against the wall before she pivoted and ducked under his still outstretched arm. "So anyway, how about that local sports team?"

"Grace."

She shook her head, her back still to him. "Bad idea, Frank."

"You told me it was okay to kiss you."

"I think I specifically said, it would have been okay if you did. If it was spontaneous, I wouldn't want you to feel bad or awkward about it. But come on, you're an emotional hot mess and I am callous at best when it comes to feelings."

"Is that true?"

"Yep, you're a total mess."

"I mean about you being callous. That hasn't been my experience."

"You've known me for three days."

"Sure, but they've been a very long three days." She heard him move, and then he was right behind her, radiating warmth against her back. "Why is it a bad idea for me to kiss you, exactly?"

"I..."

He waited.

She tried again. "You..."

"Yep. You and me. That's it. This doesn't have to be more complicated than I'm attracted to you, much to my surprise, and maybe yours, too. And I think you're a pretty safe friend to explore that with a bit. I like talking to you. I like sharing a meal with you. I think I could probably kiss you without freaking out, if that's your worry."

He thought she thought—

She whirled around, right into the circle of his arms. She looked up at him. "I don't think you're going to freak out. Not immediately, anyway."

"Maybe down the road?"

She wasn't expecting him to have that kind of insight. She stumbled over her words. "Yeah, I guess so. I'm not one for commitment, Frank. And I'm sure that's not where your head is at, at all, but you were married for a long time. It's my experience that widowers and divorced men want—"

He crushed his mouth onto hers, a hard press that stole her words and her thoughts and left her mind strangely, wonderfully blank. His lips were firm at first, commanding, but then they softened, and oh, that was very nice.

He smelled good, and the way his lips moved against hers made her scalp tingle.

And when he pulled back—just a bit—he was smiling. No regrets. "Whatever you think of me, don't for a second assume that what other men do has any bearing on my actions."

She couldn't breathe.

"Did you like that?"

"The kiss?"

He smiled again. "Yes."

"Uh…yeah."

"Good." He kissed her again. "I like you. I like that you march to the beat of your own drum. I like that you don't do commitment, or protocol, or expectations. I like *Grace*, and I want to kiss her without it being a big fucking deal."

"You swore."

"I'm a sailor. I do that from time to time. Just usually not in front of ladies."

"I'm not much of a lady," she whispered. "Feel free to say all sorts of inappropriate things in front of me."

"Duly noted." He pressed his forehead against hers. "Do you want to go for a hike with me tomorrow morning?"

She smiled up at him. "Will there be more kissing?"

"Damn straight."

"Then I'm in."

CHAPTER 8

Tegan: So I'm kind of scared to ask, but…is there
any update about Rear Admiral DeMarco? Is he
having an okay time?
Grace: Morning, baby. I think Frank is adjusting to
camp just fine. No need to worry.
Tegan: Oh, phew. Love you!
Grace: Love you, too. What are you doing up
so early?
Tegan: Last minute to-do list madness. See
you soon!

FOR THE THIRD morning in a row, Grace had breakfast with
Frank. This time neither of them approached the other. He
was waiting for her on the step when she stepped out of
her room, a big, broad form stretching the hell out of a
worn t-shirt. Her heart skipped a beat as she took in the
size of him, and it swelled in a total crush-worthy way
when he stood up and held out his hand.

Nice wasn't the right description for their walk to the dining hall. It was more than that, but she didn't poke at it for adjectives.

While they ate, he told her a bit more about the trail he'd gone up the day before, and the one he wanted to take today. Then they collected the picnic lunch he'd ordered the day before.

"Convenient that you ordered food for two yesterday," she teased him.

His cheeks turned pink. "I was planning on eating all of this myself. But I've got snacks we can add to the pack back in my room."

And so he did. After he tucked the picnic food into the bottom of a high-tech looking pack that stood all on its own in the middle of his cabin, he grabbed another bag and started unloading food. A couple of squeeze tubes, a few protein bars, and three zip-lock bags of trail mix.

He tossed one at her. "Do you like gorp?"

"GORP?" She laughed as she caught it. "Man, I haven't thought of that forever. Not since Tegan's short-lived Girl Scout days. What does it stand for again? Good Old Raisins and Peanuts?"

He snagged two protein bars and shoved the rest of the food away again. "Ah, in fact it does not."

"What do you mean?"

"That's a backronym."

"A *what*?"

He put their snacks in the bag, then pulled her close. "A back-ronym. An acronym applied backwards. Like *fuck* meaning 'for unlawful carnal knowledge.'"

73

She touched her fingers to her temples and then exploded them outwards. "Mind blown. That's not true either?"

"Nope."

"I'm the most gullible person on the planet, clearly."

He kissed her lightly. Their first kiss of the day, and she found herself leaning into it. She wanted more, but she didn't want to push him, either. His lips caressed hers and made her heart flutter in the most delicious way. "Hardly," he murmured before deepening the kiss. The barest of licks, and then a final peck. "You're fun. Don't ever change."

"Deal."

Once they ran through his checklist of things she needed to have—hat, sunscreen, good shoes, extra pair of socks—he put his bag on his back and off they went.

At first the trail was wide and easy to walk along side-by-side, but after a bit it narrowed, and they needed to move to single-file. Frank led at first, going at a slow but steady pace until they reached a plateau spot, where a few trees had fallen, creating a break in the overhead canopy. Sunlight flooded a small clearing and in this space, flowers were growing. Wild, untamed beautiful tangles of color. The Berkshires had some stunning hidden corners.

"These are gorgeous," she said, picking a few and twirling them between her fingers as Frank dug out their water bottles. She held out her hand as he handed over one of them. "Thank you."

"I saw some of those on the ridge on the other side yesterday. They're all over the place here."

"I love them." She took another long drink of water, then handed the bottle back.

As he got everything squared away, she picked a few more blooms to carry as they continued along the path.

This time she led, with Frank following closely behind. They talked a bit and enjoyed silence the rest of the time. By the end of their second leg, she was definitely feeling the hike in her thighs.

Frank gestured to a thick log. "Let's sit and we can have our lunch here," he said.

She wiggled her wildflowers at him. "But what about my friends here?"

He took them from her and slid them through the loop on his water bottle lid. "There."

"Nicely done."

The lunch was thick sandwiches, still cool from the included ice packs. Ham, cheese, tomato, and lettuce. There were also apples and a brownie for each of them, so she gave her second sandwich half to Frank. "You might need this more than me."

He pulled a knife from the side of his bag and carefully cut it in half. "How about we share it?"

She beamed at him. "Hiking with you is fun."

They took their time eating. She finished first, and Frank handed her the map so she could decide how much further they would go before turning around.

It looked like the trail opened up not that much further, and when she looked ahead, she thought she could see it through the trees. She pointed to a detail line on the map. "What's that?"

"A ridge. There's a plateau..." Frank leaned against her as he pointed.

She thought about burying her face in the warm skin of his neck, but they hadn't been that physical today. She settled for relaxing into his side. "How much further is it?"

"Probably another ten minutes of climbing."

"Then let's do it!" She jostled him, and he chuckled. "We can race."

"You got it."

FRANK HUNG back as Grace picked up the pace. He let her pull ahead. He liked to watch her move, and it wouldn't take long for her to slow down again. She hadn't been trained to keep a steady pace. Hadn't had the fun trained out of her. And that was just it—hiking with her was fun, just as she'd said. But it was her doing, not his. And just when he thought he might ask if she was tired, she'd speed up again. Bursts of speed, bursts of energy, always keeping him wondering.

It was her youthful energy that made it fun. Same as she had with kayaking, too.

They reached the plateau almost at the same time, and in front of them stretched a meadow full of the same flowers she'd picked in the small clearing.

This time, he did the picking, gathering her a big bouquet to add to the small bundle she'd carried up with her.

"I love them," she said as she turned in a slow circle.

When she stopped in front of him again, he took her in his arms.

She pushed up on her toes and they kissed. Not just once, but over and over again, until every muscle in his body was tense and ready to do more than just kiss.

He moved his mouth to her neck, then up to discover the soft spot behind her ear. Finally, he brushed a loose strand of hair off her cheek, tucking it behind her hair. "You're a bit of a wildflower yourself, aren't you?"

"How do you figure?"

"Beautiful, untamed, unexpected."

"Often mistaken for a weed?" Her eyes danced, but he heard the silent caution. *Don't try to be sweet. I don't like sweet.*

"And only romantic from a distance," he retorted drily. She laughed out loud at that, and he kissed her neck again, this time noisily. Not romantic. Just fun.

He could stick to fun for her. That wouldn't be any kind of hardship.

"Ah," she sighed, then gasped. "Oh. Frank."

Suddenly, she sounded alarmed, and he pulled back. "What is it?"

She pointed behind him.

Dark clouds were quickly gathering on the horizon. A storm was coming in and fast. It didn't bother Frank at all. He'd been stuck in a lot worse places than a meadow in the Berkshires with a beautiful and entertaining woman. But from the way a frown had settled in between Grace's eyes and how she kept glancing at the clouds, she didn't like the idea of getting caught in the rain.

It had taken them two hours to climb up. He guess-timated he could get down the mountain in forty-five minutes if he needed to, but could Grace move that fast? He wouldn't want her to try. And from the looks of the sky and the way the wind was picking up, that wasn't going to happen anyway, because the storm was moving in faster than that.

He rubbed his jaw, quickly thinking of options. "Do you want to take shelter or hoof it back to camp? We won't outrun the rain, but we might make it back before the worst of it."

"What would taking shelter look like?"

He dug out his first aid kit and handed her the silver emergency blanket. "We can use this as a tarp. If we get back under the tall trees, they'll help protect us from the worst of the downpour, too."

She didn't hesitate. "That sounds way better than running down a muddy slope."

He liked that she'd thought that far into the descent plan. "I agree."

Moving quickly, they headed back to the log where they'd stopped for water, then kept going a bit further, into the dark shadows where the trees were thickest. He didn't have rope on him, so he found a tree that had a horizontal branch nice and low to the ground. He folded the blanket over it, making a decent little tent for them. He used the second blanket from his kit to make a floor, lifting the sides up, and then they hauled logs in to pin the top and bottom together.

The floor blanket ripped twice in the process, but for a makeshift shelter, it wasn't bad.

As the first fat drops of rain hit them, they scrambled inside.

Grace started laughing as she stretched out on her back.

"Having a good time?"

She shook her head side to side. "This isn't how I expected my day to go."

"They're probably having a lot of fun back at camp."

She snorted. "Playing Spin the Bottle, most likely."

"Or Seven Minutes in Heaven."

She rolled onto her side. The storm had darkened the sky enough that once again he was having trouble reading her face. Lucky for him, Grace had no problem communicating her desires. "I bet we have more than seven minutes in here, don't you think?"

The foil blanket crinkled beneath them and the rain beat faster on the blanket above them. Neither noise was louder than his pulse as she slid into his body and offered up her lips.

He tangled his fingers in her hair and took the deep, hungry kiss she was offering.

They made out as the storm raged around them, as rain began to lash in the open ends of their shelter, and didn't stop until the emergency blanket gave up under the onslaught of heavy water against it.

With a rip, the shelter gave out, and Frank rolled onto his back, grabbing Grace with one hand and the blanket with the other. He cocooned them together as she laughed into his neck.

"Did I mention that hiking with you is fun?"

"You did," he rumbled.

She giggled. He threw his head back and joined her in the laugh, because she was right. This was fun.

He felt alive for the first time in a year, and Jesus Christ it was wonderful.

WHEN THEY MADE it back to camp two hours later, just in time for dinner, they found everyone milling around in the lobby. And for once it didn't seem like a live-action silver-haired Tinder-sponsored full-contact sporting event.

It wasn't just campers. Most of the staff were in the lobby, too.

Frank stopped the first person he recognized—Rachel from the craft building. "What's going on?"

She reached out and squeezed his shoulder, then did the same to Grace. "You didn't hear?"

"Hear what?"

"She's okay, but one of the campers, a woman named Ruth, had a heart attack this afternoon. Over board games right here."

"Oh, my goodness," Grace said. "Ruth? We had breakfast with her yesterday. She's okay, though? There's an update?"

"She's safe and sound at the hospital and being taken good care of there."

"Has someone organized a card?"

Rachel pointed to a table set up next to the fireplace.

"Over there. Everyone is signing it before you head in for dinner."

Grace grabbed Frank's hand and dragged him along. She signed her name in a tiny spot on the card, and he added his name right next to hers. Then he pulled her into his arms for a hug, because that felt like the right thing to do.

Dinner was a buffet, and they quickly grabbed plates of food, but Grace only picked at her choices.

"Are you thinking about her?" he asked.

She jerked her head up. "Ruth?" She worried her bottom lip. "I guess I am. And I'm tired from our adventure, too."

"Early night tonight?"

"Maybe, yeah." She gave him a soft smile. "Thank you. For asking, and for the day."

He reached across the table and squeezed her hand.

"You two were gone all day, huh?" A woman stopped in front of them. Frank recognized her as someone from the bus. "That's fun." She winked. "Did you get lost in the woods?"

"Got in a big zombie fight, actually," Grace deadpanned. "Took all afternoon to slay them."

Frank choked on his water as the lady gave Grace a confused look.

She just blinked innocently. "We have to get back to the battle soon, too, so…"

Frank nodded. "True story."

The woman left them alone, and he pointed to her plate. "Eat up, zombie slayer. You'll need your energy later."

He'd meant it as a joke. But Grace slowly slid her gaze to meet his and gave him what could only be described as an inappropriately dirty smile. "Really?"

His groin tugged hard. "I thought you were tired."

She lifted a meatball to her mouth. "Look. Newfound energy."

After they finished eating, they grabbed dessert to go and headed back to the cabin. As they walked down the path, Frank started laughing as he remembered the look on that poor woman's face.

"What's so funny?"

"Zombies."

Grace chuckled. "Sometimes I can be weird."

"I like weird," Frank promised as they arrived at the cabin.

She followed him into his cabin without asking. He put his lemon cake down on the table by the window and she did the same.

The heat between them ratcheted up nicely as she gave him a knowing smile.

"Sometimes I can be dirty, too," she whispered.

He groaned. "I love dirty."

"You didn't get under my shirt at all on the mountain," she said, sticking her lower lip out just enough for him to bite the pout right off her face.

He did just that, and she laughed. "My apologies for being a gentleman."

"You should apologize."

Instead, he slid his hand under her shirt and splayed his fingers wide across her warm skin, pulling her against him.

She came willingly, soft and pliant. It took nothing at all to get her on the bed, one hand up her shirt and the other roaming wild and free across the outside of her shorts.

Endless kisses and teasing touches that felt good and made his head spin.

"It's been thirty years since I did this last," he murmured as his fingertips grazed the seam between her legs. "Discovered a woman's body for the first time. You'll have to tell me if I'm doing okay."

"It's been thirty days for me," she gasped, rocking into his hand. "And you're putting the other guys to shame."

He squeezed her thigh, ignoring the way his heart beat thumped harder at that information. She'd slept with someone a month ago?

He hadn't known her then. It didn't matter.

But fuck, what was he doing? Could he compete with that?

"You stopped." She wiggled out from beneath him and pushed up onto her knees. "Why? Because I said it's been thirty days…" She jumped off the bed. "Seriously?"

His head was spinning. "No. I…"

Her eyes blazed at him as she propped her hands on her hips. "Well?"

"And I just said it's been thirty years, so give me a God-damned minute." He swallowed. Of course this wasn't going to go smoothly. He swore again, this time under his breath, and pushed off the bed.

She stepped back, and he prowled after her. Yeah, he liked this better. The push-pull tension was better than the softness they'd slipped into on the bed.

"Don't judge me," she whispered.

"Jesus, I promise I'm not. I was just worried for a minute that I wasn't going to make you feel good. That I'm out of practice compared to—"

She grabbed the front of his shirt and pulled him in. "No comparison. I promise. But it's hard to do when we're not on a bed."

He grinned, hard and feral. "Oh, my sweet wildflower, we don't need to be in a bed for me to make you feel good."

She bumped into the wall. "You aren't serious. We're too old for—"

He wasn't too old for anything. He caged her in, one arm bracing against the wall, the other hand tracing the line of her jaw as she closed her eyes. "Frank..."

"I don't care if you were with someone else yesterday. Right here, right now, it's just the two of us. And this feels right. I don't want to overthink it."

She exhaled, a breathy little pulse. "I don't want you to regret this."

Regret her? Never. "I won't. At all. I promise." And there was an easy way to make sure he could stand behind his word on that front. This wasn't going to be about him at all. He wanted to make her feel good—so good she'd want him to do it again. His pleasure could wait. "Kiss me, Grace. Kiss me and let me touch you."

She closed her eyes and parted her lips.

"You are so beautiful," he whispered against her mouth. "I can't wait to feel you come on my fingers."

He swallowed her gasp at the same moment he popped the button on her shorts. She arched into his touch and he let his lizard brain take over. Soft skin, sparse curls, and then slickness. He touched her lightly, working from the outside in. Gentle strokes until she spread her legs, then deeper exploration, dragging her wetness up to her clit and then back down again.

Not until she was begging him in panting, little breaths did he thrust a finger into her. But that quickly escalated to two, and then a teasing third as she rode his hand.

Shameless.

Beautiful.

Stunning.

His cock was leaking in his boxers as her breaths changed. Faster, more desperate. His name on a whisper, her fingers tight on his arm, and then, with a squeak, she threw her head back and everything clenched down.

Stunning.

Beautiful.

Shamelessly perfect.

"That's so good," he murmured, kissing her softly now. "So good. Yes. Thank you. Thank you..."

CHAPTER 9

It was still dark outside when Frank woke up. For a split second panic gripped his chest, but it faded as he came fully into consciousness. No, he didn't wake up because he was sad, or angry, or guilty.

It took him a minute to sort out the real reason, in part because it was a long-dormant response.

But when his cock twitched against his shorts, and he realized with a start that he was hard—really hard and getting thicker by the second—he laughed.

Fucking hell. He was horny.

Like, reach into his shorts and give himself a good squeeze, which will turn into a slow tug, and eventually get himself off kind of horny.

He wasn't prepared for this. He didn't have any tissues at hand, and he wasn't going to make a mess in camp sheets.

Closing his eyes, he cupped himself through the fabric of his shorts. *Go away,* he tried to suggest. *We can do some-*

thing about you in the morning.

But his erection wouldn't be dismissed so easily. He was thick and hard, and unbidden images of Grace wouldn't stop flashing through his mind. The curve of her thigh leading up to her bathing suit. The way her breasts were heavier in his hand than he'd expected. Her warmth and tightness against his fingers. Eager kisses. Wet tongues.

He groaned and stroked himself faster, then squeezed the crown tight. *No.* He wasn't a young buck who couldn't control himself.

That resolve lasted a minute before he was jacking his hand up and down again. Slowly this time. It felt good. She'd felt good, too.

He wanted her again. He wanted her now. Wanted to crawl into her bed on the other side of the building and wake her up with slow, intense kisses. Thrust into her and hold her down while he—

Throwing back his blankets, he stalked to the shower. He couldn't sneak into her bunk, but he also couldn't tell himself not to come right the fuck now.

There was a part of him, now awake again thanks to Grace, who was absolutely a young buck.

It took a minute for the water to heat up. He welcomed the cold sting on his back, but it didn't do anything to shrink his erection. And once the steam wrapped around him, he braced one hand against the wall and let the other squeeze his cock tight.

It was her squeak that got his blood really going. That gasping, needy little sound as she climaxed. He'd heard it and felt her shudder around his fingers. He could easily imagine how good it would feel—and sound—if her limbs were wrapped around his body and he was buried balls-deep in her pussy, too.

She was sexy as hell.

Grace Bennett. Jesus Christ.

He grinned as he remembered the smile. The zombie hunting threat. And the way her eyes flashed as she bit into that meatball. Energy. Hell, she had energy for days.

His eyes drifted closed as his own orgasm approached. His legs shook, and his balls pulled tight, then pulsed as his mind went blank. Fuck. Yes.

The release was perfect. Blissful and draining.

He stood under the hot spray for another minute, then grabbed the soap and scrubbed up as the spots in his vision receded. Maybe now he'd be able to get a few more hours of sleep.

Much to Grace's delight, Frank didn't have any second thoughts about their fling the next morning.

They spent most of the day on Wednesday making out like teenagers.

A long, breathless kiss good morning before breakfast. A secret press-against-the-wall in the boathouse before kayaking. A gentle brush of lips-on-lips, right out in the open, before a picnic lunch on the lawn.

They even had a mid-afternoon nap together, their clothes staying on, because there was a special evening entertainer that night—an illusionist, which sounded quite excellent.

That night, Heather Tully waved Grace over as they entered the amphitheatre for the magic show. "Hey," she said breathlessly. "So, this might be good news, if you're interested in surprising Tegan and Wyatt. This guy happens to be free tomorrow night. He's not heading on to his next gig until Friday. So if you wanted to hire him for a second show tomorrow night, for the early wedding arrivals…"

The camp director kept talking, but Grace stopped listening. A loud buzzing had taken over in her head. Her daughter was arriving tomorrow. She'd just gotten Frank halfway past second base, damn it.

Priorities, Grace. Right.

She smiled graciously at Heather. "That sounds fantastic." It did. Just…their time together was coming to an end just as it got started.

"Are you okay?" Frank asked as they settled into seats halfway back from the stage.

She nodded. What could she say that wouldn't come off as clingy?

He kissed her cheek, and she focused her energy on that. The sweetness of the moment, the promise for the end of the night.

Soon the lights dimmed, and as dramatic music started, they came back up, revealing a man in a tuxedo in the middle of the stage. He introduced himself as the Wicked Maestro. "Or Wick for short. I'll also respond to Maestro, and Hey You if you're holding a twenty."

The room chuckled.

"Or even a crisp one. Let's be honest, I'm easy if you want my attention. Now who here has been to a magic show?"

Frank leaned in, brushing his lips against Grace's ear. "With a crowd this age?"

Everyone's hand went into the air.

Wick cleared his throat. "Okay, so I've gotta do some new tricks. Err...."

That got another laugh.

And sure enough, his first couple of illusions were ones Grace had seen before. A floating table, a couple of card tricks. But then he surprised the crowd with some unexpected tricks, many of them pulling people from the audience.

Grace found herself clapping and laughing along. "He's good," she murmured to Frank.

Wick disappeared behind a screen, then came back juggling two balls and a...gun. An extra long one. Not quite a rifle, but longer than a pistol. Shocked reactions and nervous laughs rippled through the audience.

Grace shared their surprise, her whole body tensing up.

"That's a paintball gun," Frank said quietly in her ear.

Oh, well that was better than a real weapon.

"And for my next trick," the illusionist said as he continued to juggle. "I need a volunteer who knows their way around firearms and is used to taking orders. Because I need someone who will, on my order, shoot me right in the face." The crowd gasped. "Is anyone here a police officer? Anyone with military training?"

Grace pivoted her head towards Frank. His neck darkened just above his collar, and she jerked her attention back to the stage, but it was too late. Wick had noticed, and whoever was operating the lighting had as well. A spotlight landed on Frank.

Wick came closer. "You, sir. Are you a police officer?"

Frank cleared his throat. "Navy."

"Excellent, excellent. Come with me, if you don't mind. You're just the man for this trick."

She felt Frank's discomfort viscerally. *I'm so sorry*, she thought. He reached over and patted her knee, giving her a half-smile before standing up. "We need to work on your poker face," he murmured.

"You don't need to do this," she whispered up at him.

"It's fine. If the man wants me to shoot him with a paint pellet, who am I to say no?"

She still bit her lip.

But as Frank strode to the stage, her nerves on his behalf fell away, and she sat back in her chair. It was hard not to appreciate his presence. His grace for his large size, the way he commanded the stage. She could imagine him in his uniform, but even out of it, with a few days of camp scruff on his jaw and wearing nothing more than a faded t-shirt and cargo shorts, he looked in charge.

The magician—who had requested Frank, after all—even looked a little nervous.

That's right, buddy, Grace thought. *You want him to shoot you in the face. Crazy pants.*

Wick explained to the crowd that what he was going to hand Frank was not a real gun, but a paintball gun, which

Grace already knew. Then he showed everyone a single paint round and handed it to Frank. "Write your initials on that for me, sir."

"I don't have a pen." Grace hadn't heard that voice before. It must be Frank's Rear Admiral voice, and it was very intimidating. It also made her a little tingly in her middle-aged lady garden. That's right. Frank's don't-fuck-with-me voice made her want him to fuck-with-her all night long.

Wick laughed nervously. He handed over a sharpie, and Frank scrawled sharply on the ball. Wick took it back, loaded the weapon of his destruction, and handed it over.

Frank immediately settled back into an expert-looking stance. Grace noticed he kept the gun pointed at the floor, the muscles in his forearm flexed.

It was hard to pay attention to the rest of the illusion when that forearm was on the stage. She knew what the golden hair dusting his skin felt like under her fingertips, and what those muscles could do to her body.

The magician handed Frank something else. A paper target to shoot through. Grace missed why, but it didn't matter. Wick was giving Frank a countdown now, and with impressive precision, Frank readied his weapon and on command, pulled the trigger without flinching.

The whole room gasped.

Wick wobbled.

Frank stood stock still, the gun pointed right at Wick's head.

And then the illusionist turned, opened his mouth, and

showed the crowd a bright blue paintball caught between his teeth.

He pulled a ziplock bag from a pocket, spit the ball into it, and jogged across the stage to Frank. "Trade you," he said, his voice shaking.

Frank didn't break a smile. "Sure thing."

"Can you tell the ladies and gentlemen in the audience if those are your initials?"

Frank looked at the plastic bag, then raised it over his head. "They are."

The audience erupted with applause, and Grace's cheeks hurt from grinning.

CHAPTER 10

FRANK WATCHED the rest of the show with his arm wrapped tight around Grace. When it ended, she had to disappear for a minute to confirm with Heather that the guy would be back the next night for the wedding guests, and then she was all his.

He took her hand and led her out the side door, away from the crush of campers returning to either the main lodge for more partying or the cabins beyond.

"Let's take the long way around," he said, squeezing her fingers gently. "It'll take a bit longer, but we won't have company on the walk back."

"Now that you're famous for staring down a magician, that's a smart choice," she teased.

"You liked that?"

"I loved it. I was worried at first, though. I'm sorry for giving you away."

He laughed gently. "It's fine. Really. I don't mind."

She stopped and reached up, touching his neck. "Your neck turned red. I thought you were embarrassed."

"Oh, my sweet wildflower, I don't embarrass *that* easily." He caught her hand and kissed her fingertips. "Can I tell you something personal?"

"Of course."

"Bianca used to notice the neck thing, too. It usually means I'm happy. Sometimes it's a tell if I know I'm going to be good at something."

Her mouth dropped open and her eyes sparkled. "Really?"

"Yep." He set his mouth, trying hard not to smile back. He failed.

"That's kind of neat. And here I took you for an introvert."

"Like you?"

Her mouth quirked to the side. "You figured that out, huh?"

"Kind of obvious. But no, thirty-seven years as a career officer in the United States Navy. Any natural introverted tendencies I may have once had have been drummed out of me."

"I guess so."

"I don't like people right now because I'm—" He cut himself off. He'd been about to say he wasn't happy, but that wasn't exactly true. "Because I spent a long time stuck in grief. And terribly unhappy."

"Of course, you did. I remember—and I'm not saying it's the same, at all—but after my divorce, I went through a grieving process of my own. It lasted for *years*. I probably should have gone to counselling or something, but instead I poured myself into planting fields of lavender."

"That sounds like pretty good therapy to me."

She smiled, and he realized with a start he was hoping she might invite him to her farm.

Instead, she turned and started walking again, tugging him along. Fair enough. They hadn't talked about anything beyond camp. And really, they hadn't talked about camp itself. They'd simply gravitated toward each other and now he couldn't imagine not seeing her again after the wedding.

But maybe that was a problem for tomorrow.

Tonight, he wanted to make her feel good.

"What are you thinking about?" she asked, glancing at him sideways.

"The future," he said simply.

"Post-retirement?"

"I guess so."

"What are you going to do next?"

"Nothing."

She waited.

He laughed. "I'm only partially kidding. I honestly have no idea how I'll fill my time."

"Can I give you some unsolicited advice?"

He lifted their entangled hands and kissed her knuckles. "Of course."

"Everyone needs a purpose, Frank."

He'd had two. He'd been a husband and a SEAL, and nothing else had mattered. He took a deep breath. "I know. I'll find my way."

He hoped.

The trees grew thicker as the path curved away from the buildings. He wrapped his arm around her, encouraging her to lean against him. "Thank you," he whispered. "That's good advice."

"I know a little something about being lost, and I can't imagine losing the love of my life." She squeezed her arm around his waist. "But the man I saw tonight...he'll figure it out."

That was the thing. That man? He was mostly an act these days. "I'm not sure he's real," he confessed.

"How about the man on the mountain yesterday?"

He'd been real as anything. Frank hauled Grace hard against him and crushed his mouth against hers. "He's legit," he growled.

"Then trust him." She kissed him back. "Race back to the cabin?"

GRACE WAS glad she'd worn running shoes. Frank let her win, but not by much. He caught her around the waist as she leapt onto the porch, and the next thing she knew he had her pinned against the door on her side of the cabin.

"Again with the fun," he rumbled.

"That's me, Little Miss Sunshine," she said breathlessly.

He groaned and pressed his mouth to her neck, sucking on the skin there. "My wildflower," he whispered. "But yes, sunshine, too."

"My bed or yours?" She tried to quip it, but it came out quite serious.

He didn't seem to mind. His hands tightened on her body and he dragged in a rough breath. "Yours."

The room was dark, lit just from the moon, but they both knew where the bed was. Grace fell back with a sigh as Frank climbed on top of her, his thighs pressing hers apart. He trailed his fingers down her neck and over her chest, palming one breast as he took the other nipple in his mouth. She rubbed his cheek, the rough stubble a shocking contrast to the soft, wet heat of his mouth.

Melting into the mattress, she let him be in charge. He kissed her roughly, then softer, pausing here and there to check that she was still with him.

Oh, she was so with him it hurt.

She needed him inside her pronto, but the man hadn't done this in more than a year, and the last time had been with the love of his life. Grace could be a little patient.

And worst-case scenario, he'd do that thing with his fingers again and she'd be just fine.

Slowly but surely, they lost items of clothing. His shirt first, then hers. Then her shorts, and she was in her underwear for a while. He kissed every inch of exposed skin until she was squirming, and then the rest of the clothes went poof.

When he was back on top of her, Grace lifted her hips, needing him to fill that ache, and they both shook when her wet sex made contact with his erection.

"Condom," he muttered, but she was way ahead of him. She'd already opened a box earlier that day, anticipating this moment.

"Under the pillow," she gasped.

"Genius woman." A quick rip of a packet later he was sheathing himself and then he was right there again, notching into her.

She moaned his name as she arched toward him, and he braced his arms around her.

"Grace," he whispered, his voice shaking.

She cried out again as his first thrust stretched her to the aching point. Stretching her arms above her head, she fisted the pillow in one hand and scrabbled at the solid headboard with the other. Frank tipped her hips up with one wide hand curled under her bottom and found her wiggling fingers with the other hand. She curled her legs up high on his side as they surged together like that, hands clasped, and bodies entwined.

She'd fantasized about him on top of her all day. The reality was so much better. She couldn't keep her mouth off his skin, kissing his mouth and his neck and his chest. She desperately wanted to take a bite out of the bulging muscle where his neck met his shoulder.

The whole time he kept moving inside her, relentlessly building that unbelievable feeling that she just might explode from desire. "So good," she panted, and he lifted his head.

"Tell me what you want." The room was nothing but shadows, but her eyes had adjusted, and she could see the intensity on his face. Even if there had been any doubt, she could hear it in his voice.

"This, I just want this." She tightened her legs. "You inside me."

His face twisted, desperate need warring with astonishment, and then he groaned. Deep, feral, perfect. She would remember that sound for the rest of her life and hold it like a secret treasure.

"Frank." She said his name on a long breath, then again and again, chanting it as he tilted his hips, finding her clit between their bodies.

"Come with me," he said, his voice tight as his body shook over her, and she ran her hand over her belly, down to where they were joined. The hot, wet spot where he filled her, and then she closed her eyes, tipped her head back and pushed herself over the edge as he exploded inside her.

CHAPTER 11

FRANK HELD Grace as she fell asleep. He dozed off, too, but not for long.

It had been too long since he'd slept next to another body, and the last few times had been agonizing. This—not the sex, but this quiet period after it—was the unexpected trauma he hadn't seen coming.

After a while, he got up and carefully dressed, then stepped outside.

He didn't go into his own cabin. He wouldn't be able to sleep if he did, and he had had enough of lying miserably awake for a whole lifetime.

He sat on the step.

Their step.

In a few short days, it had become a place where a lot had happened. Now he let those memories wash over him. Not just things that had happened at the cabin, but up on the mountain. On the lake. And then something she'd said after he'd helped her get back in her kayak.

When they'd taken their drinks to the sunny patch of grass behind the main lodge and learned a bit more about each other.

The start of their friendship in a lot of ways.

"Better something than nothing."

She'd been talking about travel. About grabbing what you can afford, what was available, rather than bemoaning that it wasn't exactly what you wanted.

But it felt hollow inside to think of grabbing a person, knowing they were only something, and not everything.

Bianca had been his everything.

Grace could never—

Frank groaned, a loud, guttural wounded sound. He was the worst kind of monster for even having that thought.

Grace was amazing. On every level, she was a fantastic woman. She deserved more than sharing space in his head and his heart with the ghost of a wife he'd adored for three decades.

"Can't sleep?"

He jerked his head around and saw Grace in her doorway. She was in her oversized pyjamas again and looked cute as hell. She'd dressed herself before coming to find him.

He'd left her naked in her bed, and she'd had to put on clothes because he'd snuck out. Sure, he hadn't gone far, but still...

Guilt swam in his gut. "Yeah."

"Do you want company? Or would you prefer privacy?"

"Company," he said without hesitation. But then he

winced. God, he couldn't keep his shit straight. After two days of being fine, now was not the time to fall apart.

She didn't react to his facial expression. Maybe she couldn't see it in the shadows. "'Kay."

He swallowed hard. "You should go to sleep, actually."

A beat went by, then another, before she softly said, "Are you feeling guilty?"

"You don't really believe in personal boundaries much, do you?"

"Highly overrated. Unless they're mine, in which case they're sacrosanct. It's a weird thing of mine."

"You have a lot of weird things that are actually pretty sound. I'll trust this one, too." He took a deep breath. "Yeah, I'm feeling guilty. A bit."

"I know you miss your wife. That's okay. I've been with widowers before."

He laughed and groaned at the same time.

She was undeterred. "At our ages, Frank, we all have baggage. I don't trust men as far as I can throw them, and with these pipe-cleaners—" She flung her arms wide. "That's not far at all. But everything you've shown me this week says that you will be straight up with me. That's all I ask. Maybe we should have that old-fashioned conversation about intentions—because I don't have any beyond getting laid."

Her words echoed between them as she fell silent.

Getting laid.

He was twisted up about space in his heart and she wanted to use him for his body. What the fuck was wrong with him that he couldn't see that?

"I don't have a lot of emotional bandwidth to share," he said quietly. "But I appreciate the hell out of you. I see you as someone who deserves the moon, and I feel guilty that I can't be the one to snag it for you."

"That's what you feel bad about? Not…" She trailed off.

He shook his head. "Bia wanted me to be happy. To death do us part. That was our vow. I took it well past that point, but I need to start living again."

"You do." She smiled softly. "I'm happy to help with that. Fair trade for orgasms." She straightened up. "I'm going back to bed. If you want to join me, it might be nice to wake up together. And if you need some space, that's fine too. Of course it is." She leaned in and kissed his cheek. "But that was amazing. And I'd happily do it again."

So would he. He caught her wrist. "I don't want to hurt you."

"You can't." She smiled down at him. "Do you want me to wake you up with sex in the morning?"

What kind of a question was that? He pushed to his feet and followed her back to bed.

As PROMISED, he was dragged out of slumber by a whisper and a teasing, light touch of fingers along his jaw.

Bia, his brain thought at first with a confused jolt. Then he remembered, and instead of guilt, he felt a strange floating feeling. He frowned, trying to make sense of it.

"Wake up, Grumpy Pants," she murmured. "And gently, please."

He harrumphed. "You just called me grumpy."

"I like grumpy." She slid her hand under the blanket, her fingertips spreading that lovely, floaty feeling across his whole body. "Mmm. But I was wrong about the pants. I like this better."

"You stripped me of those last night. And then…" He cracked his eyelids and focused on her smiling face.

"And then, indeed." She stroked his thickening length. "And now?"

Now he felt…

Peaceful.

And ready for more of this woman. Immediately.

"Climb on top of me," he said, his voice rough with need.

"I was thinking of something else." She wiggled down his body, her breasts brushing his chest, then his thighs as she settled between his legs, the blanket discarded off the end of his bed. "How do you like your blow-jobs?"

"However you want to deliver them," he said huskily. Was she for real? And were people picky about getting their dicks sucked? Because he was happy for whatever.

"Sloppy, fast, and with some friendly help from my hand."

"Jesus, do you go out in public with that mouth?" He brushed his thumb against the corner of her mouth. "Whatever you want, wildflower. Whatever you want. Please. Anything."

"You're babbling, Frank."

"It's early. I haven't had coffee. And you're kind of blowing my mind."

"Not yet," she whispered, her breath brushing the head of his cock. "But I will be in three, two, one…"

And she did.

It was exactly as promised. Sloppy, fast, and with very clever help from her nimble little fingers. He came hard, spurting his come across her tongue before he could warn her it was coming.

She licked her lips like a happy little kitten anyway.

He let out a helpless moan and hauled her back up his body, kissing her hard on her talented mouth before she nestled into his side.

"When I first met you, I thought you were delicate."

She snorted.

"I get now that that's not accurate."

She rolled onto her back and stretched out. He loved how uninhibited she was with her body. With sex and laughter and teasing. She looked at him and shook her head, making her breasts jiggle. "Not accurate at all. You can't hurt me, Frank. I'm tough as nails."

"I know," he whispered, climbing on top of her. The sensitive crown of his cock dragged against her skin, and he thought about staying there until he got hard, thought about fucking her senseless until he could pour himself into her again.

But they had breakfast to get to. A second breakfast, in a way, because he was going to feast on her just as much as she had on him.

And then it would be a countdown until they lost their privacy. His SEAL team would be arriving later today, along with Grace's daughter. For the rest of the weekend, it would be hands off.

Mouths off.

He dropped his head and tasted the skin at the base of her neck. God, that was going to be hard. He loved the way she tasted in the morning. And at night, after a day in the sun.

From a distant recess of his mind, a warning whispered. *Don't get too close*, it said. He licked his way over her chest to her nipples, ignoring the suggestion from a well-meaning but too-cautious part of his brain.

Life was short.

Grace was fun.

He was going to enjoy the hell out of her in the time they had.

He tasted his way down her body, and when he settled between her thighs, he gave her *his* specialty. Slow, teasing, and worshipful. Her legs wrapped around his head when she came, flooding his mouth with her unique flavour.

And as he pressed his forehead into the crease between her thigh and her hip he realized it was way too late. He was already painfully close to this woman. He was already invested. And at some point this weekend, he'd need to steal a moment of the mother-of-the-bride's time to talk about his big plans to go down on her again in the middle of a field of lavender.

CHAPTER 12

THE FIRST WEDDING guests to arrive, mid-morning, were Elaine and Brian Henderson. Wyatt's parents had driven straight through the night, according to Brian.

"It's a seventeen hour drive we made in sixteen, didn't we?" He looked at Elaine, who nodded, then back to Grace.

She didn't bother to tell them she'd abandoned her car in New Hampshire. She was pretty sure the Hendersons—who were lovely people—wouldn't find that funny in the least. "That's impressive," she said instead. "Do you know Frank?"

"Admiral," Brian said, holding out his hand. "A pleasure to see you again, sir."

Oh. So it was like that.

Grace took a tiny step away from Frank. Rear Admiral DeMarco for the rest of the weekend, she supposed.

He gave her a small smile. Yep. And so it began.

The next to arrive were Grady and Priya Mills. They'd met through Tegan and Wyatt two years ago, and also fell in love at camp. Priya was a news producer and Grady was a SEAL. They hadn't come with the rest of the group flying in from out west, though, because Priya had worked all week in Miami. Grace hugged her tightly. "How are you? I heard you had some flight troubles."

"All's well that ends well. I'm here now, and that's all that matters."

"Tegan's so happy. Did you text her that you'd arrived?"

"I did."

"Good girl."

Then it was Grady's turn for a hug. Grace had only met him once before, but she hugged everyone. He was gracious about it.

The last arrival before lunch was Grace's ex-husband, Charles Bennett, and his new wife of seventeen years. Not really new, but the word had stuck in Grace's head. As long as she didn't say it out loud, it was fine.

FRANK HAD DRIFTED AWAY for most of the morning, but as soon as Charles arrived, he was right back at Grace's side.

He knew she wanted space and wasn't sure about people seeing them as overly familiar, but damn it, if this man stressed her out, Frank would be there to sooth that wound.

Except Grace and Charles got on just fine. They were pleasant to each other, and not just in tight, careful ways. They had an extended conversation about the illusionist that night, and the rehearsal dinner the next night. Charles asked about the other campers, and Grace reassured him the wedding parties would take place in relative privacy in various places around the camp property.

It was surprisingly healthy.

Frank almost left her to it, but then Charles and his wife excused themselves to go check in to their cabin, and that's when Frank saw it.

Grace sagged.

Just a little. Just enough for him to notice, and maybe nobody else would. Her ex certainly didn't, and Frank noticed that the man looked back at Grace.

But Frank saw, and he didn't like it.

Catching Grace by the hand, he tugged her into the shade beneath a big oak tree. "Are you okay?"

"Sure."

"Really?"

She stuck her tongue out at him. "Yep."

"Your ex seems pleasant."

She sighed. "Yeah. Okay, so he's a handful and I've learned how to manage him over the years and that's exhausting."

"I thought so."

"Thank you."

He glanced around. They were alone. He cupped her face in his hands and kissed her gently. "Lean on me whenever you can this weekend."

She breathed in deeply. "I'll try."

"And don't ever change. Not for him. Not for anyone."

This time she kissed him.

That was the last alone time they had that day. After

lunch, Tegan and Wyatt arrived with a good chunk of SEALs, and it was Frank who was whisked away by his men. He caught Grace's gaze as she swept her arms around her daughter, and then it was a few hours of beers and stories with a good group of young guys who cared deeply about his well-being.

"I don't know if I appreciated your thoughtfulness enough before I flew out here," he said gruffly. He hadn't appreciated it when he'd arrived, either, but he kept that part to himself. "But this week has been good for me. And I'm already over my jet lag, which is quite nice."

They all laughed at that, but he was serious, and he told them so. It was a day for gratitude, and he was taking that seriously.

But after dinner, when all the greetings were over, and the group was getting comfortable with each other, the solemnity passed. As the illusionist began his show, Frank knew exactly who to push up onto stage when it came time for the paintball trick.

"Wyatt," he said, leaning forward to clap the groom on the shoulder as everyone gasped at Wick, juggling the paintball gun with those balls. "Put your hand in the air."

"Sir?"

"Trust me," he said quietly in the SEAL's ear. "This is going to make Tegan's night."

Wyatt's hand went into the air. *Good man*, Frank thought. He was going to make a good husband for Grace's daughter.

Tegan squealed as the magician picked her fiancé to join him on stage, and she gripped her mother's hand as

Wyatt did exactly what Frank had done. He followed the man's instructions, trusting that it was an illusion and nothing more.

But if the guy wanted to get shot, a SEAL would make that happen.

When Wyatt returned to his seat, everyone applauding enthusiastically, Grace shot Frank a knowing look.

He grinned.

After the show drew to a close, people drifted off in different directions. Frank headed to his cabin alone, but he didn't go to bed. When Grace made her way down the path forty-five minutes later, he was waiting on their porch. "Did you like that?"

She stopped in front of him. "I don't think I've given you enough credit for your sense of humour."

He smiled faintly. "Maybe I haven't shown enough of it to you."

"Want to take me to bed and show me a bit right now?"

"Nothing I want to do to you in bed is funny," he protested.

"I bet we're going to laugh," she said.

She was right.

CHAPTER 13

FRIDAY NIGHT, Tegan slept over in Grace's cabin, so the mother-of-the-bride didn't get any late-night laughs with her secret boyfriend. It was a worthwhile sacrifice to cuddle with her daughter one last time before her baby got married.

The next morning, they did yoga at dawn, then got pampered by a crew of people who came in from Briarsted.

By the time the photographer arrived to document their progression to the ceremony site in the woods, Grace was super emotional.

"I'm not going to cry," she said bravely.

"Mom, your cheeks are already wet," Tegan whispered, leaning in to kiss one of the tear-streaked patches.

"Damn it." Grace dragged in a breath. "I told myself I wasn't going to do this. And here I am, and it's just…you're so beautiful, baby."

She really was. Tegan had picked a lightweight wedding dress that moved like the wind as she followed the photographer's instructions. First, they stood together at Grace's cabin on the porch, mother and daughter smiling brightly to stave off threatening tears. Tegan's hand found Grace's and squeezed tight. Then they moved toward the path leading into the woods where the ceremony would take place. The photographer had Tegan stop in a sun-spot, where the golden streams of light made her glow.

Her floral crown, which replaced a more traditional veil, and Grace's daughter looked every inch a truly-in-love woodland nymph.

Then Tegan's dad appeared at the top of the path. She ran to him, and Grace let them have their moment, their set of photos together before she caught up.

When she fell into step on Tegan's right, Charles looked over at her and smiled. She was shocked to see his eyes were wet. For all that she didn't understand this man, they shared an elemental emotion today. Their baby, who had grown up a long time ago, was now starting her own family. They were officially done being her immediate, primary unit.

They had never been a conventional family, not even before the divorce. Charles had always worked in the city and they'd only ever had a piece of him. Once she'd moved upstate it had become official. He'd taken Tegan on holidays and paid for her to come to Camp Firefly Falls.

Two decades later, this place was changing Grace's life in the most unexpected way.

She smiled back at her ex. "Ready?" she asked Tegan. "I think your groom is waiting for you."

Tegan took a deep breath and linked her arms with both of her parents. "Let's do this."

FRANK STOOD next to Wyatt's parents. They were good, honest folks. Farmers from Wisconsin who hadn't been enthusiastic about their son's choice to join the navy, but today they couldn't look prouder. Elaine's eyes were bright with tears, even as she beamed, and Brian kept giving Wyatt a thumbs-up.

The wedding would happen in the center of a circle of people. Right now, there was a gap at the trail head, where Tegan and her parents would appear momentarily. Her two bridesmaids, Molly and Priya, were waiting on either side of the space, ready to close the circle tight once the bride arrived.

A speaker lodged in the crook of a tree played a simple instrumental piece. Flute music which fit the setting perfectly.

In Frank's experience, SEALs tended to go in one direction or another when it came to getting married. Dress uniforms all the way—like he had done thirty-three years earlier—or not a single military reference anywhere to be seen. Henderson had gone that route, and it seemed to suit the couple. It also suited the setting.

All the men were in suit jackets, although not all wore ties. The groom and his two best men were in khaki. So was his father. Frank had gone with a navy-blue suit himself—and the tie was tight, as it should be.

He'd been touched when Elaine Henderson gave him a flower for his label that matched her husband's. "You've been like a father to our son for more than a decade," she'd said. "When we weren't sure what he needed, you led the way. We'll always be grateful for that."

Now she let out a small gasp, and Frank followed her attention to the trail. The first thing he saw was Grace, and for a beat, she was all he *could* see. She was breathtaking. Her blonde waves were pinned up and back, with delicate flowers tucked into her hair. They matched the ones on his jacket, and his chest pulled tight.

Then he turned his gaze to her daughter. Tegan Bennett had always impressed him. Smart, lovely, and kind. Today was no different. She shone as a bride, with flowers in her hair and a beaming smile that completed the gorgeous presentation.

One day, she would look just like her mother. Wyatt was a lucky man.

Heather Tully stepped forward. "As a newly licensed marriage officiant, I am thrilled to guide Tegan and Wyatt through their commitment ceremony today. Two years ago, this couple met here at camp, and as they have moved toward this moment, they have thought long and hard about what it means to marry each other. For that reason, they have chosen to write their own vows. Please join hands and give them your heart-felt energy as they commit themselves to each other in blessed matrimony."

Frank took Elaine's hand on one side, and Grady Mills' on the other.

In the center of the circle, a tough-as-nails Navy SEAL

took hands with a hippie girl and his voice cracked as he started to recite vows he'd clearly memorized. "I, Wyatt, take you, Tegan, to be my wife. I promise to stand by your side through life's ups and downs. Through tough times and joyous ones, too. I will celebrate all of your successes, support you in everything that you do, and never let go of your hand when things get hard. I will be your mate. You have my heart."

"I will protect it," Tegan whispered back, but the words still carried through the clearing. "With everything I have. And you have mine."

"I will protect it," Wyatt said gruffly. "With everything I have."

"I know you will." Tegan smiled a million-watt grin. "I, Tegan, take you, Wyatt, to be my husband. I promise to stand by your side through life's ups and downs. Through tough times and joyous ones, too. I will celebrate all of your successes, support you in everything that you do, and never let go of your hand when things get hard. I will be your mate. You have my heart."

Heather raised her hands in the air, and as one, the group did the same, a circle of fists drawing up to the sky. Before Frank could react one way or the other to the intense woo moment, it was over. The camp director-turned-wedding officiant exhaled and dropped her hands, a glorious smile on her face.

Sort of like a prayer, he guessed. He could roll with that.

"Tegan and Wyatt, you have exchanged vows from the heart. Let these words be your guiding path as you navigate the world together, hand-in-hand. Know also that you are surrounded by a powerful circle of friends and family. Lean on them in difficult times. Trust them to support your marriage when things get tough, and celebrate your successes, just as you will do so for each other. Marriage is a vital pillar of your community, and your community is a pillar in your marriage."

It was true, Frank realized with a jolt. He'd always thought of his marriage as an island, his refuge from the intensity of his career. But Bianca had been there for his SEALs and their spouses, and when things for tough for him, his SEALs had been there for him.

Tegan and Wyatt kissed, a sweet, long embrace that everyone cheered, then the delicate flute music returned, and they were showered with flower petals as they took to the path, leading a procession back down the trail for their lunch reception and an afternoon of dancing and drinking.

He found himself drawn to Grace as the circle dissolved.

"That was beautiful," he said, meaning every word.

She waved a handkerchief at him before tucking it into an invisible pocket in her dress. "I know!"

He chuckled and leaned in. "You look lovely, by the way."

She blushed.

Would they ever get a chance to have a public relationship? Frank wasn't sure if he ever wanted to get married again, but Heather's hippy-dippy words about marriage and community had him thinking.

And all of his thoughts right now were about this blonde pixie beside him.

"Could I have this dance?"

He'd been eying her for an hour. There was not a single cell in her body that wanted to deny him this request, and so she didn't. Maybe it was the champagne talking, or maybe she just really liked Frank so much she wanted to dance with him. "Absolutely."

"How much wine have you had?"

"Not enough to crawl into the wrong bed," she said primly.

"Enough to crawl into the right bed?"

"Definitely."

He chuckled as he turned her around the dance floor.

"Are you having a good time?" she asked.

"I am. I really am." He sighed contentedly. "This week ended up quite differently than I'd expected."

"For me too." She said it softly, but there was no masking the wistfulness in her voice. Damn it, champagne. That was not the influence she'd been looking for.

"This doesn't need to be goodbye."

She'd been thinking about that. It didn't need to be. But maybe it should be. It would be easier that way. They could forever think back on this week as a lovely moment in time.

"Grace?"

She couldn't say anything. Couldn't say those thoughts,

couldn't bring herself to hope that maybe she would see him again and they could keep exploring whatever this was between them. "Tonight," she whispered, not meeting his eye. "Let's talk about this later."

"I want to talk about it now."

"But I don't know what to say," she admitted, the words tearing from her chest in a panic.

He stopped in the middle of the dance floor, took one clear look at her face, and led her out of the tent and around the corner of the boathouse.

"Frank—"

He cut her off with a kiss, hard and unexpected, his hands on her face first, then pushed back into her hair. He held her still and tasted her over and over again, before finally pressing his forehead hard against hers. "I don't know what to say either, wildflower. It's okay. We'll figure it out together."

"This was just a little fling—"

"Not little. No matter what, don't diminish what this was."

"But I don't know what it was," she whispered. That was the truth. She'd held on for dear life while the universe whipped her and Frank into a lather, and now that it was done, she wasn't quite sure what had happened to them.

Something lovely. And he was right—not little at all.

"It was an ambush," he murmured. "We didn't see it coming."

"That's for sure."

"I want to see you again. I know what it is to only have

memories, Grace. I don't want to cling to memories when someone good and real could be in my arms instead."

She dragged in a deep breath. "Maybe when I come out to visit Tegan…"

"Or I can come visit you. I'm retiring in a month, and I'll have a lot of free time on my hands."

"I'd like that."

"Me too." He brushed a light kiss against her forehead. "You make my heart feel whole again, Grace. That's important. I don't want to push too hard, but this week healed me, right here." He took her hand and pressed it against his chest. "Thank you. Again. Always. Thank you."

CHAPTER 14

October
Saratoga Springs

GRACE PUT the last of her new batch of soap in the cupboard, where it would cure for the next six weeks. It was quitting time. Her assistant had left an hour ago, but she'd wanted to get a bit more work done while Frank was busy outside.

She tidied up, then went to the kitchen and grabbed two bottles of beer from the fridge.

He was at the back of her property chopping wood. He'd been doing it daily since he arrived, and at this rate, she'd have enough split logs for the next three winters. He'd even dragged her, albeit willingly, to the home improvement store yesterday so he could get a better ax. Something about a man needing a proper tool to get the job done right.

When she found him, she watched him work, because he didn't look up.

He was a machine.

"I have beer," she finally said.

He split one more log. "Excellent."

"I'm worried about you."

He set the ax down slowly and hung his head. "I'm sorry."

"It's okay," she said softly. "You can tell me what's wrong. I won't be upset. Is this too much? Too fast?"

He lifted his head again, his mouth hanging open. "Shit. No, Grace. God, that's not it at all. I'm sorry because I wasn't clear enough that I'm just fine. I'm happy. I've thrown myself into splitting all your logs because it feels good. That's all."

Relief coursed through her. "Oh. Oh! That's great!"

He smiled gently. "You were worried about me." A statement. A soft, happy statement.

"I was. I am."

"I worry about you too, but I wasn't sure that was allowed."

She laughed. "What do you worry about?"

"You not having enough logs split for the winter, for example."

"I'm probably good now. And I can always order a cord of wood if I haven't—"

"Why would you do that when I could—"

"Because—"

They stopped at the same time and just looked at each

other. Then Frank sat on the stump, his ax clattering to the side. "Come here, woman."

She laughed as he tugged her into his lap. She handed him his beer and they clinked bottle necks together.

"I want to get your firewood ready," he said gruffly. "I want to be around a lot this winter, and I'm a weak California boy, so we're going to need a lot of fires to get me through, you hear me?"

"I hear you," she whispered. "I like the sound of that."

"Do you? Good. Sometimes I'm not sure."

She sipped her beer. "I'm sorry."

He kissed her. He tasted like beer, and she liked that a lot.

"We need to talk more," she murmured.

"I spent thirty years with Bianca figuring out my strangeness and translating it into human. I'm out of practice in having to say things out loud all the time."

"It's been twenty-five years for me." She sighed. "We're quite the pair, aren't we?"

"Maybe that's why we work."

"I guess so."

"I know what I want," he said quietly. Assuredly. "I've been thinking about it a lot."

"Me too. Both on the thinking and knowing." She pulled back enough to make sure he could see her face. "I want you around a lot this winter, too."

"And when the snow gets too cold, you can come to my place in Coronado. You've got a daughter to visit, she's a good excuse."

She cupped his face with her free hand. "I don't need an

excuse to come and visit you, Frank. And I can stay at Tegan's house if that's easier."

"I said what I said. I want you to come to my place. I want—" He took a deep breath. "I want to split wood here. I want to fix your bookcases and build you new ones. I want to show you my life, my home, and share it with you. I want you to bring life back to Bianca's books, and not because they were hers, but because they've sat still for more than a year and you'll love them."

"I know you will always miss her," Grace said. It was important to say that out loud.

He nodded. "Forever. But when I hold you in my arms, I'm not thinking about her *like that*. It's not a comparison thing. Ever. I love you, Grace. Exactly as you are, exactly where you are, and on your own terms. I want to share my life with you in a way that makes you happy. Visiting back and forth for now, and then one day, when you aren't looking, I may just move in for good."

"But California—"

"We'll keep my house. We'll want to visit the kids. But you built all of this, and I would never ask you to leave it. Besides, I look really good in flannel."

"You do." She laughed and tugged at his collar. "I'll have to get you more—"

"Did you hear me?"

She had. She was still processing it, so—

"I love you." This time, he didn't say anything else around it.

Harder for her to ignore this way. She saw what he was doing. So she nodded.

"I didn't think I would find love again. But I have, and it's different with you. This thing between us…it took me by surprise."

"You said it was an ambush." She finally found her voice. "At camp. That's what you said when I said I didn't know what this was."

"We were ambushed by love, because neither of us thought it would happen for us again. And then bam, it did."

"I'm set in my ways," she murmured.

"I'm not looking to change anything about you. I want you exactly as you are."

"But with a better book organization system."

"Not even that. Just more shelves. I love the precarious piles. Let's just get them up off the table, so I can cook for you."

"So much pressure," she grumbled, and he laughed as he squeezed her tight.

EPILOGUE

April
Coronado

"Happy birthday to you, happy birthday to you, happy birthday dear Mom..." Tegan and Wyatt were louder, but as they sang, Grace saw Frank mouth her name. *Gracie.* Somewhere over the winter holidays he'd added the -ie to her name and it had stuck.

She blew out her candles in a single breath. It helped that there were just two of them, a wax number five and a wax number six.

"Thank you, my darlings," she said as she served four big pieces onto plates. "So far, this has been a magical birthday."

"And you haven't opened your presents yet," Frank said, grinning. He'd already given her a card, along with breakfast in bed—and an orgasm to start the day, too. But he'd kept the big present a secret until the kids arrived for cake. It was in the living room, a large box wrapped up in bright yellow paper. It had been there since she'd arrived three days earlier.

They'd been flying back and forth regularly, with Frank staying with her in Saratoga Springs more often than he was here in California. But two weeks ago, he'd flown out west ahead of her, saying he had some birthday preparations to take care of.

She was pretty sure the present was handmade, and that warmed her heart more than she'd ever have expected at this point in her life. Or any point in the past.

Frank was more than she'd ever wanted, and everything she would ever need.

He was even better than the birthday cake Tegan had brought, and that was saying something. "This cake is incredible, baby. Where did you get it?"

"This bakery I found near the—" Tegan stopped and looked at Wyatt. "Let's give her the card now."

He laughed and kissed his wife on the head as he got up to grab an envelope they'd set on the sideboard.

Grace took it from him, curious as she ripped open the flap. Inside was a birthday card. Bright green and pink. Very cute. And then she started reading it.

What's the best way to say
Happy birthday?
Is it with a kiss, or a hug,
Or a cuddle with a bug.
What's the best way to celebrate

Is it balloons or a nice big cake?
So when it's Grandma's day—

Grace's eyes filled with tears and she put the card down, her hands shaking. Tegan flew into her arms and they hugged each other tight.

"Really?" she whispered into her daughter's hair. "A baby?"

"Yep. Just before Christmas, I think."

"That's wonderful news. So, so wonderful." She breathed in deeply and squeezed Tegan tight. "How are you feeling?"

"Just fine. Really, so good."

When they pulled apart, she saw Frank was shaking Wyatt's hand. She smiled at them. Frank would be a grandfather. What a special gift that would be.

He caught her eye, and she crooked her finger at him. He came close and gave her a gentle kiss. "Big news," he said softly.

"I know. Grandma. Nana? Granny? I can't choose."

He laughed out loud. "I don't think you need to pick right now. And I've heard the grandchildren sometimes have a say in that, too."

"I suppose they do." She squeezed his hand tight. "What about you? What do you want to be called?"

He shrugged one of his big shoulders. "Just Frank, I suppose."

"Oh, no," Tegan said, throwing herself around him. "You're definitely a Papa. Or maybe a Grampa."

"I don't know..." His neck turned red.

A year ago, Grace would have wondered if he felt uncomfortable. Now she knew that meant he was pleased. She squeezed his hand. "Definitely Papa."

He smiled. "We'll let the munchkin decide that." Then he cleared his throat. "Okay, my turn for gift giving. Let's go through to the living room once we've finished our cake."

Grace stood up, giving him a smacking kiss on the cheek. "Cake can wait. I want to get into that present! It's been teasing me since I got here."

They paraded into the living room, where she took a picture of the giant present before hooking her finger under the yellow paper and ripping it back.

Inside was a piece of furniture. It looked like a desk, of sorts, but higher. A standing desk, maybe, with lots of drawers and tiny shelves.

"It's a cross between a potting bench and an apothecary table," Frank said, wrapping his arm around her. "I was hoping you might have a reason to spend more time out here, and you'll need a work space to make soap and try new recipes, even if the primary work happens back in New York."

"Oh, Frank," she breathed. "It's magical."

"And when the baby arrives, we can make more changes to the house, whatever you need."

She stopped poking into the various nooks and crannies and gave her love her full attention. "Frank."

"Yes?"

"You are the reason I would spend more time out here.

Not just the baby. I'm thrilled about the baby, of course I am, but you are my heart. You are enough to make me endure this constant sunshine and golden sand."

"Me?"

"You."

"Well how about that."

"I love you, you big, gruff man. I love that you made me this table, and I love that you're excited about being grandparents together, and I love that you don't want me to ever change."

He swept her into his arms and buried his face in her neck.

She squeezed him tight.

"I love you right back," he murmured against her skin. "I can't wait to be Grampa to your Grandma."

Her heart skipped a beat.

She brought her lips to the curve of his ear. "We're going to make that dirty, right?"

He chuckled under his breath. "You know it, wildflower."

KEEP READING with other books in this series by Zoe York. Skinny Dipping Dare (Tegan and Wyatt's book), Take a Chance on Me (Grady and Priya's story) and Winning Back His Wife (Heather and Michael Tully's book) are all available.

Sign up to get mail from camp when a new release comes out!

www.campfireflyfalls.com

ABOUT THE AUTHOR

Zoe York lives in London, Ontario with her young family. An author of more than twenty sexy small town and military romances, she is a fan of heroes that could be swoon-worthy in real life, and heroines that could be her best friends. She's currently chugging Americanos, wiping sticky fingers, and dreaming of heroes in and out of uniform.

Website: www.zoeyork.com
Newsletter: www.smarturl.it/ZoeYorkNewsletter

f facebook.com/zoeyorkwrites

twitter.com/zoeyorkwrites

instagram.com/zoeyorkwrites

COPYRIGHT